Sassy, Sexy, and Stalked

SHELLEY K. WALL

Cover Design and Interior format by The Killion Group
http://thekilliongroupinc.com/

DEDICATION

To all you wonderful readers that take the time to read my work and appreciate it. Thank you!

And to my family for putting up with all my lofty dreams, no matter how silly they may seem at the time.

DISCLAIMER

OTHER TITLES BY SHELLEY K WALL INCLUDE:

Numbers Never Lie
Bring It On
The Designated Driver's Club

For a more current list, go to www.shelleykwall.com

CHAPTER ONE

Reva Zamora shivered from the chill that always rushed over her when Adam Huber was around. Why was he so creepy when the rest of her coworkers thought he was practically a saint? She realized she shouldn't be judgmental. Her counselor had told her she needed to stop distrusting the world, or in this case, him. One bad experience from the past shouldn't be allowed to taint future ones.

She hadn't been able to cross that bridge.

Instead, she stopped seeing the counselor. Her instincts had always served her well in the past. They saved her life in fact. She decided to trust them more than a complete stranger that used statistics versus personal knowledge. How could she possibly understand what Reva had been through?

Adam looked over his desk with dead eyes, "Have you ever used a gun for therapy, Reva?"

The desk was piled high with paper and electronic parts. His computer monitor glared from behind him, framing his solemn face in a blue glow. The picture was nothing less than eerie, made even more so by his question. She assumed that was why he had asked it.

"Not really, but I own a gun," Reva chose not to admit that it had never been used, and she was thankful it had not. There was a time when it was her closest companion and the fear that drove the purchase had weighed heavily.

She recognized something when she glanced over his

shoulder at the blue screen. Icons. She narrowed her eyes and focused. Her desktop. Adam had remoted into her desktop, and opened her files. He was snooping through her employee data. It was there plain as day.

"You want to tell me what that is?" She pointed at his screen, trying to ignore the hairs on her arm that prickled as she raised it.

"Work." His voice held a ting of challenge. He pressed a couple keys to engage the screensaver.

"I doubt that. Exactly what do you need with my computer, especially my employee files and where do you get off snooping through them without my knowledge or approval?" She felt a flush coming up her neck but she sucked in a breath to maintain composure. She hated it when her old fears started to take hold again.

"That wasn't your computer and I wasn't snooping. H.R. asked me to do some research for them." He stood, bringing his eyes level with hers. He lied.

The screensaver scrolled a line across and he looked down at his desk, tapping fingers on a printed picture that held his interest. "You ever used that gun of yours, boss?"

The chill in her arm spread through her back and Reva rolled her shoulders involuntarily. *Was he threatening me?* "Who exactly asked you to do this 'research'?"

Adam walked around his desk, brushing against her in the confined space, his face within inches. He ignored her question. "My counselor said I should take up a sport or hobby. Said it would take my mind off things."

She had no idea how to answer *that* and his acrid breath against her arm further added to the chill. "What things?"

"He said it would give me an avenue to express my stress in a positive way."

"So, you chose weapons? That's positive?"

"There's something exhilarating about punching holes in a target until it's completely obliterated." His voice hissed. "I imagine the face of my latest problem as I fire it. It's – relaxing."

"Would that really be considered a sport?"

His face twisted into a grin. Reva stood to her full height, attempting to gain control. She recognized the menace in his actions but she had just discovered an employee snooping on her computer. That was a violation of policy. He could try to avert her attention with scare tactics but she'd not fall for it.

"I don't see what that has to do with your connection to my computer and I seriously doubt Human Resources would authorize you accessing your supervisor's or anyone else's without consent. Who did the request come from? I'll call and check."

Adam lowered his head and softened his voice further. By the time he spoke it was so quiet, the threat of his words hung in the air like smoke in a bar. "I told you that wasn't your computer. You never answered my question, Reva. Have you ever used that gun of yours? Have you ever felt the thrill of blowing the hell out of a picture that represents whatever makes your life miserable at the time? You answer mine. I'll answer yours."

In past years, she could have held the bravado easily, because it had been a core part of her. Recent years had taught her to keep it hidden. Silence it so that one didn't cause further anger or aggression that might end up in –pain.

She backed away, and turned, her focus on escape, aware her trembling was visible.

He laughed. Not a scary laugh that fit the craziness of his prior words. A *normal* laugh that seemed to dispel the fear. "I'm messing with you, Reva. Here, I'll call upstairs and you can talk to them. They'll confirm what I told you."

With his hip on the corner of his desk, Adam lifted the receiver of his desk phone and finger dialed an extension. He lifted it to his ear and waited. Reva thought it odd how quickly he had transformed from threatening to casual.

A couple seconds ticked by.

While he waited another call rang through, summoning him to answer. He feigned disappointment. "Voicemail. Sorry." He clicked to the other call before she could ask him to leave a message. When he answered the other call, he turned as if dismissing her and began a conversation with the caller, apparently a girlfriend. He mouthed the words "excuse me" and waved.

.

CHAPTER TWO

———   ———

Two days later, Reva's blood boiled. She almost heard the bubbling and she definitely felt it. If anyone walked down this hall, she was certain they'd turn and run after one look at her face. *Did Adam just call me a lunatic?*

She heard the words from the other side just as she pressed palms against the cold wood to open the door of the staff room. She was seconds away from trouncing in, but decided to take a few breaths instead. *Practice your yoga breathing.* She attempted to calm herself. This came from a staff member with no experience that she'd hired away from a local restaurant. He had practically begged her for the job and she'd taken the chance against her better judgment. *He doesn't have the nerve to talk to me in person?*

His words continued on the other side of the barrier, speaking to an unknown listener. "I mean, did you hear her talk in the meeting yesterday? She has no idea what she's doing and she's so inconsistent it's ridiculous. I absolutely hate her. I swear to God, I felt like punching her when she spoke but –,'" she overheard.

"That's a little over reactive," Gavin, one of her other direct reports, responded.

"I'm not really the violent type anyway."

"I don't think she intended to upset you. She's just trying to give you direction. Maybe the *way* she says things could be nicer."

Nicer? I practically coddled the guy because he's so moody and I didn't want to offend him. She smiled. *So much for the breathing exercises.*

"It's not just that. I can take constructive criticism as well as the next guy. I'm not that sensitive - but she's so harsh – her words aren't the problem. It's how she uses them. The tone. And those incessant lists she makes are annoying. Does she do that when you're talking to her, or is it just me?"

The faint smell of McDonald's fries reached her nose. Gavin often ran through the drive-thru on his lunch hour. She knew this because he offered to get her a burger whenever he went.

Gavin ignored the question and laughed. "So, you're telling me if she said the same thing all soft and sweet, you wouldn't have a problem?"

"No. Um. I guess. Yeah."

"Better check your gender bias, man. If a guy said it, he'd add a damn or something, or call you a few names – and you wouldn't give a shit about it. Besides I think her intention is good – she's just saying what's on her mind. She's trying to do her job. If you have a problem with it, tell her. She'll listen."

"Maybe I will."

"Or quit and find someone you can deal with."

"Where would I go? Besides, that's too drastic."

Reva jolted back to the present when the clip clop of approaching heels caught her attention. This was probably *not* a good time to stop in and check on Gavin's projects as she'd intended.

Later at her desk, Reva rubbed her throbbing temples. A quick glance at the clock signaled the weekend was upon them and she could go home. More time to consider how to handle what she'd learned. As she drove home to the suburbs, she debated that logic too. After all, if he was that unhappy, surely she should talk to him and find a way to resolve the problems right? Although if he intended to talk with her, he would. Left unattended, his foul mood was certain to infect the staff in a negative way. If he said all that to Gavin, what else was he complaining about, and to whom?

"It doesn't matter," she said out loud. "Anyone who knows

me will take it with a grain of salt. You can't change opinion by attacking it. Just keep a positive face on and it'll all blow over."

Reva knew why he was upset. She had caught him trying to log into her computer again...he had denied it. She knew that denial to be untrue but couldn't prove otherwise. Apparently, he didn't care for being caught red-handed. Responding by suggesting that she should try to find a boyfriend rather than follow him around didn't exactly lighten her mood. Especially since she *followed* him right into her own office. The opposite mood resulted, in fact. The word "fired" flashed through her brain but she bit it back.

That was the old Reva. She was determined to be a better, more street savvy woman going forward. She seriously knew she could turn him around – he was a talented young man that worked hard and could change his attitude. She was certain, or at least she had been before hearing his conversation with Gavin, now she wasn't as confident.

She shrugged and wished she could tell the truth to Gavin to clear up why Adam was complaining, but that was out of bounds. Never discuss employees with other employees. She considered going to Human Resources. Her old self would have stormed in earlier and fired him on the spot.

But her old self had been taught a lesson –that self was too brash and prone to spur of the moment decisions. At least until her mouth put her in acute care with stitches. No, it's a minor issue – it will turn out fine in no time. Besides, she had no intention of appearing incompetent as a manager by taking every little squabble to someone else for resolution.

By the time Reva reached her house, she'd convinced herself to leave it alone and move on to happier things. This was an exercise she had undertaken often over the past few years just for self-preservation. She sighed. An abusive relationship will do that to a person.

Her thoughts derailed when she walked up the sidewalk to her front door and viewed a very fine looking stranger lazing across her step in shorts and a brown t-shirt. That certainly brought out the happy. The chacos on his feet looked worn and, judging by the tan lines on his toes, they'd seen heavy use. The prickle of fear that had always hit her when surprised was short-lived. Apprehension was forced away as she mustered a slight smile, yet held her breath. She really wanted her old self back.

"You live here?" he asked, squinting into the sun behind her as he stood.

Reva debated answering. He didn't *look* dangerous but then neither had her ex-fiancé. She shook her head

"No? Do you know who does then?"

She gained control of her voice and answered, "Yes, I'm sorry. It's my house. Can I help you?"

"I live back there." He pointed straight through the house. "Behind you."

"Ah. You're the one who keeps throwing lemons and limes over the fence. I've been meaning to talk to you about that. Can't you just put them in the garbage or something?" *How does one politely tell a person not to use their backyard for disposal?* The first time fruit had sailed over the fence, it had terrified her such that she ran inside and locked the door. Subsequent discoveries of lemons and limes gave way to irritation that the yard had become a dumping ground for her neighbor's unwanted harvest.

He laughed. Actually, he sparkled. Weird. "I throw them over to all my neighbors. I thought you might like them and I've got too many. Listen, my son's ferret crawled under the fence and it was in your backyard."

"Oh, no problem...come on. You can go through here and get it." She strode to the side gate and opened it, waiting for him to enter. He stood back and motioned for her to proceed.

"Not really necessary. He climbed over and got it himself," he said.

She glanced over her shoulder puzzled, but kept moving through the fence with him following. "I don't understand."

"He broke some yard-art thing you had back there when he crawled over." His footsteps plodded closely behind her. Oddly, the hair on the back of her neck had not risen. Yard-art. That was a good way of describing the welded contraption her brother had gifted her with on her twenty-ninth birthday. It always required an explanation – it was intended to be some sort of sundial, made of metal with a ceramic globe in the center. She had never known what to do with it so she put it at the back of the yard, out of the way for mowing. One of many.

"It's a sundial," she stated. The shards of ceramic lay in the grass like a cracked egg. Ben will be pissed. Ben believed in hand-made gifts, never bought any, and he took it personally if the new treat wasn't proudly displayed. Her backyard had metal art in every possible opening.

"Wow," the man said when he saw the conglomeration of metal, glass, and rocks sprawled around. "Either you're really into your yard or your husband's really into welding."

"Neither. My brother makes this stuff and I don't know what to do with it. He gives it to me all the time. I can't just..."

"Say no or throw it away? What a softie," he teased.

"Yeah, but I draw the line at the front yard. At least I have standards. I'm not putting any of this stuff out there." She reached down, gathered the fragments of ceramic and started toward the trash. "Don't worry about this. As you can see, there's plenty more." She waved a hand at the other items.

"Still, this one was unique. I'll get you a new ball for it." He walked over to a table that Ben had made of metal and concrete. "This is cool. Your brother did this too?"

"Yep. Not the chairs, just the table."

He stood over it, shoulders square, tanned arms and legs, admiring the work. As he leaned down to smooth fingers over the surface, Reva noted the tightness in his arms and legs. He worked outside. Or he's a fitness buff. He turned suddenly toward her and caught her eyes...on his butt.

"Nice table." A slow smile warmed his face. He rubbed a hand on his shorts and held it out. "I'm Todd Grisham."

She hesitated, then shifted the ceramic pieces to one hand and grasped his. "Reva Zamora."

"Well, Reva. Where would I find something like that?" He pointed to the pieces. "Unbroken, of course."

"I said don't worry about it. You don't need to replace it." She dropped the pieces in the trash and brushed her hands together.

"You have to help me out on this. I'm trying to teach my son a lesson on taking responsibility. He's the one that will replace this, not me." He lowered his brows into a frown. Todd had an interesting face. His nose was straight and long with a small scar at the side. A shadow of whiskers lined his chin and one eyebrow had a small bare spot, very likely another scar. She doubted those marks appeared in the same manner as the one on her left temple just below the hairline.

"I see. Well, in that case, your wife can probably track one down. I'd imagine they have them at a craft store or garden center. I don't really know."

"That'd be tough. My *ex*-wife just dumped Eric on me so she could spend the weekend with her ex-boss, whom she's banging and plans to make hubby number three, hence the ex-wife. I doubt she'd be much help. And personally, I'd rather not ask her."

"Oh. Sorry."

"Don't be. Ancient history. It's been two years."

"Not that ancient. How old is Eric?" She realized he would notice the quick calculations going through her head. Two years divorced, kid of....

"Five."

Five years. So, married seven?

"Eric is from her previous relationship but I'm the only dad he's known." Todd's face went serious as he explained. Oh, well, that completely blew the calculations out of the water. Reva frowned but listened. "I'm lucky she lets me still see him. It'd be pretty hard on him to be ditched by two dads."

"Does he remember his real dad?" She squinted into the last glimmer of sun that dipped behind her roof.

"Barely, but he's awfully young to deal with that. As far as I'm concerned, he's mine. I've fed him, stayed up all night with him when he was throwing up...and taught him how to pee like a man."

Reva smiled. "Well, that would certainly qualify you."

He flashed another quick grin. "Life's important lessons. Anyway, she's not exactly the ideal mother. I should have seen that from the beginning and taken it as a sign."

Reva cleared her throat and turned to the gate. "At least he has you, right?"

"Yep. Every other weekend he has me...plus whenever she

doesn't want him." He picked one of the broken pieces of ceramic from her trash and followed. "You like to jog, don't you? I think I've seen you on the roads."

"I run in the mornings before work and at least one day on the weekend. I started a few years ago. It keeps me sound – physically and mentally." Once the words were out, she wished to take them back. Too much information.

"Usually does. Although it's probably not a good idea to run so close to the center. Do you play sports?" She turned when he asked and caught his eyes on her hips. The quick shift startled him into meeting her gaze. "Payback." He shrugged. "Don't tell hubby."

"None to tell. I played softball and ran track in high school. I haven't done much since. Why do you ask?"

"I saw a sign at the pool that they're starting a softball league next month. You might like to play." She wondered if he had signed up.

"I'll keep that in mind."

"Well, I need to get back – my neighbor's with Eric. See you." He waved and sauntered toward the corner. Reva watched for a few seconds, and then internally scolded herself for salivating. She checked her neighbor's doors. Had anyone noticed them? Once inside, she realized she hadn't flinched or jumped even once in Todd's company. Must be a good sign things were getting better. Right?

Days later, Reva plodded down the center of the street two blocks from her home and thought back to the interaction with Adam. She accepted that she had likely made more of it than necessary. Her morning runs invigorated her, lightened her mood, and even the conversation between Gavin and Adam was dismissed as trivial gossip. She chided herself on her ability to make too much of an incident and continued to work diligently with her staff on their projects. She was excited at how quickly some of them moved and although Adam's seemed to have slowed significantly, she expected that he eventually would work out whatever roadblock was causing him trouble. No need to interfere at this point.

When Friday afternoon arrived and he still had no progress to report, she admittedly was concerned but didn't want to confront him yet. Reva had one golden rule when dealing with staff—one passed on to her by a prior supervisor. He had been a business professor in a previous life and studied the psychology of business closely. The rule was: give praise and reward any day of the week, but never give criticism or correction on Fridays. Most people will stew over it all weekend and come to work useless or angry on Monday. Not to mention the dent in productivity it would make. Mondays and Fridays are usually the biggest catch-up days, so let them concentrate on those efforts.

Reva had jokingly questioned his logic, but he gave her resources to validate his suggestion. After checking them and the research behind his comment, she put it into practice and found it to be fairly accurate. Of course, there were some exceptions when it wouldn't fit but for the most part, it helped. Truthfully, she hated confrontation anyway, but those days were worse. So, she made a note in her calendar to speak with Adam Tuesday morning about his project and left to enjoy the weekend. She shrugged it off when he completely ignored her wave as she passed his door on the way out.

CHAPTER THREE

———   ———

It wasn't often that Reva woke on a Saturday morning with absolutely no agenda whatsoever. It was a well-earned luxury since she had stayed up past midnight working, cleaning the oven, doing laundry, and vacuuming. These sudden bursts of energy were hormonal, no doubt. Regardless, she lay in bed, stretching from head to foot, with a lazy grin of satisfaction.

"How on earth will I spend the day?" she asked out-loud. Glancing at the open closet which stared at her with invitation, the black shiny bikini purchased less than three weeks earlier almost waved. She nodded. "Of course." After all, the weather girl projected unseasonably sunny weather and there wasn't anyone to stop her. Why not take advantage? She padded to the bathroom, scrubbed her teeth, washed her face and doused herself in sun lotion before donning the black summer buy.

The annoying ring of her cell reached out as she lazily ate toast and sipped a morning cup of coffee. Reva sighed at the display and cursed, then thanked, the gods that blessed her with a big family.

"Have I caught you doing anything illegal?" her sister, Maria, asked.

"Eating breakfast. Does that count?" Reva chewed into the phone. Maria always asked the ridiculous just to get a reaction.

"Only if it's laced with something interesting. Want to go shopping this afternoon then over to Mom and Dad's for the barbecue? Mom wanted me to ask."

"Is Mom buying?" Reva loved it when her mom got a generous streak and a lonely one at the same time. Reva always got at least one good outfit from it.

"She said she'd spring for some sexy tops if it would help the dry spell."

"Gee, thanks. Even my own mother thinks I can't get a date. Remind her that I'm not an old maid yet and that sometimes being choosey is a good thing. How would she feel if I'd gone through with the wedding to Nick?"

Reva took a swig of coffee as the phone fell silent. She knew her mother was likely listening – she always did. For some reason, the woman loved to have everyone on the same line and just enjoy the sound. Maria said it made her feel like old times at the house but Reva suspected she was just nosey.

"I realize you all think that a nice man will cure me of Nick's influence, but personally I'd prefer no man at all right now. I'm gonna hang here and do some sunbathing but I'll come by for dinner. Give me a rain check on the rest."

"Got it. And don't mention that jerk's name again. We're all glad you figured him out and sent him packing. Or rather packed yourself and hauled butt. How's work going?" *Figured Nick out?* Maria really didn't know everything apparently. Reva wondered if her Dad had admitted to the phone call Reva made that night. The night she'd ran home to Papa like a baby. It had been almost impossible to speak with her eye swollen shut and her lip feeling like a smashed banana. Still, he'd called the Police and Nick had been jailed long enough for her to get out. Leave it to Dad to sugar-coat what really happened.

It was great how Maria turned the conversation away from anything that might upset her. She had a knack for doing that with everyone in the family.

Reva called her *the mediator* behind her back—and to her face sometimes. Just when they all started flaring up in their Latin-induced emotions, she would dampen it with a completely off the wall subject change that effectively squelched a brawl. Sometimes it would make Reva want to deck her—as she had always loved a good argument—until recently. And their family certainly had some.

"It's work. Same old. Same old."

"Rev, I think you could possibly have the most boring job ever. No wonder you never meet anyone interesting. They're all nerds like you."

"Yes, but they're nerds with a good job that comes with a decent salary. Besides, who wants to date anyone from work? That's asking for disaster. I can just see me getting involved with someone, eventually sleeping with them, and then going to work and going – 'oh, you again.' – and having to pretend I don't know absolutely *everything* about him. No thanks." A small choking noise on the phone confirmed that indeed her mother was listening. "Oops, sorry Mom. I mean, it's not like I really ever do that anyway. So, don't worry."

Maria rushed a "bye" then hung up.

Reva grinned at the cell as she hit the end button. She loved to give her mom a little bit of a heart palpitation in the morning. That always got the juices flowing and served them right for interfering.

She dropped to her feet, grabbed the towel she'd brought with her and found her favorite sunny spot in the middle of the yard. With the radio blaring, Reva settled her sunglasses on her face, and promptly returned to a half-sleep with her toe tapping to some pop song she'd never heard before. A few years ago, she had been very comfortable nodding off in the sunshine. Not now. A half-sleep that periodically included her eyes skirting around the yard was the best she could manage.

A bug landed on her leg. She twitched lightly to send it away but it returned in seconds tickling softly against her shin. After the second twitch yielded no results either, Reva glanced down to send a hand swatting the insect away. At the sight of a furry length of rodent that seemed ready to either crawl onto her or take a bite, she let out a scream and jumped to her feet. She watched as the potential neck-warmer scurried toward the back fence and slithered through a space where the grass had been dug away. *That must be the kid's pet.*

A dirty face peered through a knothole in the wood. "You okay ma'am?"

She quirked her head sideways and met the small eye with a curious gaze. "Are you Eric?"

"Yeah. Sorry about my ferret. He likes to eat your plants

and sometimes I can't catch him before he makes it under the fence." She heard some rustling around as the kid climbed up to peer over the top of the fence at her. "You going swimming?"

Reva looked down at the swimsuit and shook her head. "No, just sunbathing." She reached for the towel to wrap around her.

"Don't stop on our account." A husky voice joined the child's. Reva jerked her head up and caught Todd dropping an arm over the fence, watching her fumble. "He has Bugsy back in the cage so he shouldn't bother you anymore." He had a shit-eating grin sprawled across his face and she knew he'd witnessed her bolting up when she felt the animal on her leg.

"Does it bite?" She ignored him and wrapped the towel around her waist. She wanted to wrap it around all of her, but she decided against it. She wasn't that squeamish...or prudish either. With the towel covering her hips, she dropped her hands to her waist.

"Only if you antagonize him. He's usually pretty skittish himself so he just runs off most of the time." Todd had dirt on his hands; a small fleck of it fell to the ground.

"Today's a yard work day, hmmm?"

"Fillin' holes," Eric answered. "Bugsy keeps digging under so we're fillin' 'em up."

"Oh. Thanks for that." She smiled.

"Then we're going to get a new ball thingy," he added when Todd nudged him.

"Thanks for that too, but—"

Todd cut her off. "Eric's going to pay for it himself with the money he makes working in the yard today. After he fills the holes, he's adding some plants to try to deter Bugsy from getting through. Aren't you buddy?"

"That's right. Better get back to it." The child gave a dirty-handed wave as he dropped behind the fence.

"Sorry we bothered you, Reva." Todd pulled his arm in and smiled. "Nice suit, by the way. Should get a lot of attention at the pool—you might want to tie those strings up though." He disappeared behind the fence to join Eric.

Reva looked down and let out a gasp. She had loosened the strings from her neck so she wouldn't get tan lines. Great! I almost flashed the man's five-year-old son. She yanked the strings tighter and cemented them in place. Tan lines will just have to do. Her old top had been a tube-like thing and she didn't think about the strings.

She settled back onto the towel and closed her eyes but the sound of the voices on the other side of the fence held her interest. Would it be obvious to mute the radio and listen? She guessed so. Still, a few words came across and it was entertaining to hear the number of questions Eric asked and the calm way Todd answered them. Her brother's kids were much the same way but she hardly ever saw them.

Reva lounged in the warmth of the sun and fantasized about tan legs and worn-out chacos sitting next to her. It amazed her that she had been able to relax knowing they were just past the fence. Still, something about their presence relaxed her further and she felt the pinch in her shoulders release along with the tension in her neck. She drifted off with a smile on her lips. Incredibly realistic footsteps plodded her way. Thump. She sucked in her breath and jolted up, then rubbed her eyes to get the blinding brightness into focus. When she moved her hands from her face, a cardboard box lay next to her full of lemons and limes. She blinked up into the sun, placing a hand above to shade her view.

"I didn't want to toss them and hit you. Throw them away if you want but they make great lemonade. I use the limes for some pretty killer mojitos." Damn those legs. She quelled a rash impulse to reach out and stroke the baby-fine hairs and toned calves.

"I love mojitos. You'll have to give me your secret." She glanced at her watch and realized she'd been in the sun almost an hour. "Wow, I'm going to be toasted. I fell asleep." She knew he didn't understand the importance of that statement.

Todd smiled and reached out a hand to help her up. "You were drooling. If I'd been a burglar, I could have robbed you blind." Or worse. He pressed an index finger to her arm and pulled away. "But it doesn't look like too much sun."

"Thanks to SPF 50 and my very kind genetics." She stared at his hand briefly then took it and pulled her towel up with her, wrapped it around, and tucked the loose end. She noticed

Eric surveying the contraptions surrounding the yard with interest. He hesitated to touch, but with hands in pockets he shuffled through the grass, curiously eying the various pieces. She warmed at the small man carefully evaluating the engineering and creativity of her brother's artwork. Reva slid her eyes back to Todd.

A slight twitch lifted his brow. "Kind genetics," he repeated.

Reva felt the sweat trickling down her spine and decided to make a graceful escape and clean up. She pushed hair away from her forehead noticing the dampness there as well. "Thanks for the fruit. I'll have to try the mojito thing. That sounds great. I need to get going."

"Oh, sure. Big plans for the weekend, I guess."

"Family dinner at the parents." She grimaced. "Not exactly what I'd call big plans but with a family like mine it can sometimes get that way."

"You must be from around here. Don't tell me. You grew up here and have never lived more than fifteen minutes from Mom and Dad."

Reva didn't care for the tone in his voice. Accusation dripped from his words as if she had no adventure in her. If only he knew. At one time adventure was her middle name. Put a capital A on it and serve it up with a little fun too. Okay, maybe that was overstating a bit. Doesn't matter. That was the person she had been once, not now.

"Nope. I grew up in San Diego. My Dad's military. He transferred here when I was fifteen. I was furious that my entire social life had to be uprooted for his job." She swept a hand up to wipe the drip of sweat trailing down her chin. "I have a sister and two brothers, all of whom can drive a person to drink. The oldest two were already gone by the time we moved. So, when I was eighteen, I decided to do what a very driven but sanity-seeking high school graduate would do. I went to college in Florida and got an MIS degree. Then I missed everybody - so when a job opportunity came up here, I tried for it and got it." Not to mention that I wanted to get as far away as possible from an abusive ex-fiancé.

"Your parents must be proud."

"Hardly. Our family is full of various levels of achievement and my little degrees are the least of them. That's what happens when you get a bunch of hot-headed siblings competing against each other."

Eric called out to Todd. "Dad, you could sell some of this stuff. Don't you think?"

"Funny, that's what I thought when I saw it too." Reva turned and watched Eric run a finger over the table Todd praised earlier. "I have an internet-based lawn and garden sales business. We have a few stores but most of our stuff is sold over the internet."

"Wow. That must be a lot of work."

"It can be. I like to be outside so at first it was a hobby while I ran a landscaping business. People liked the originality of the pieces I added to their yards and a friend suggested I should sell them. It all blossomed from there and now I don't do the landscaping unless it's for a friend or one of my old customers – or right here." He waved a hand at the back fence. "And I'm inside a lot more than I like with all the work required, but it's still fun."

"I'm burning up so it's time I headed inside myself. Thanks again for the limes." She waved as he started back to the side gate. She should probably get a gate lock so people wouldn't tromp in and startle her. She watched the flex of his calves as he moved and shrugged. Maybe not. That was one of the things she loved about her parent's neighborhood. All her high school friends had been pretty welcome to come and go as they pleased, along with most of the neighbors. There was always something going on in someone's yard, and it was assumed that the neighbors were always welcome. A peeping tom or stalker wouldn't stand a chance in their crowd. Of course, there were downsides too – like people always in your business. Something that had encouraged her to get away. Plus whenever weekend barbecues rolled around, people cooked twice as much food as needed so then even more were asked along. There was little room for dieters. These were more like block parties than backyard barbecues. "Hey, you and Eric want to come with me to the dinner?"

She put a hand to her mouth as if to draw back the words. It was a completely involuntary move, asking like that. Still, it came out as naturally as asking Maria would have. Odd.

"Nice of you to ask but no, thanks. It's a family thing. We shouldn't intrude."

She laughed. "You don't know my family. We love intrusions. Besides, this is more like a neighborhood thing. There will be a crowd there and definitely lots of kids Eric's age. It won't be awkward if that's what you're worried about. No one will make any sort of assumptions about us." At least, I hope not.

He met her gaze. "I wasn't worried."

Eric ran up to grab his hand. "Can we go, Dad? Please?" The child really had the puppy-dog eye thing perfected. Reva could see it wasn't lost on the man either, which warmed her heart. The wind blew a waft of lemon-lime fragrance between them. The exchanged look between the two was almost comical, a Dad wanting to please his child but caught in an awkward situation. The boy's facial expression tugged an involuntary laugh from Todd and Reva both.

"Don't you think it's impolite to invite ourselves to someone's family get-together?" Todd placed his hands on hips and fake-frowned.

"If you had invited yourself, that would be the case—but you didn't," Reva corrected. "I wouldn't have asked if I thought it an issue. I'm not that nice." She grinned.

"Could have fooled me," Todd said, "but I can see I'm severely outnumbered on this, so we'll go. You're sure it won't be a problem?" He closed the distance between them, hands in pockets.

"Not one bit." Reva nodded and gave a conspiratorial wink to Eric.

"Hey! It would be nice if someone didn't fall for his game. I hate to see what will happen when he's a teenager. At least let me have a little bit of control over this situation, please. What time should I pick you up?" He leaned toward her and lowered a teasing brow in mock admonishment.

Reva stared at six feet plus of solid strength and testosterone. The likelihood anyone would be able to push Todd to do something against his will was non-existent. He was a softie with the kid, an appealing trait in her eyes, but he wasn't a pansy. The jovial attempt at intimidation encouraged a laugh from her and as she let it go, another strange feeling crept in behind it—warmth that wasn't sun-induced. Although every inclination was to step into the man, she took a deep breath and backed up. She rattled off a time and escaped to the comfort of her house.

CHAPTER FOUR

———   ———

It wasn't often that Reva's family showed surprise. When Maria brought home the short-term boyfriend who spent evenings and weekends in a theatre troupe, they'd barely given him a glance in his made-up white face and red lips straight from a performance. Reactions were a bit more noticeable when Tim was babysitting his neighbor's toy poodle and carried it to the house decked out in its own shoes and silk bows. He stuffed the tiny dog in his shirt pocket and calmly took the few jibes he received later in the evening. His only response – "Cute girl, cute dog." Ben, the eldest, made sure his kids fed it lots of jelly beans which left a trail of colorful stains on Tim's shirt before it upchucked all over the silk bows.

Reva's confidence that Todd and Eric's appearance would warrant little more than a glance was quickly lost when they arrived. Her mother dropped the beer she intended to hand to Reva's dad. Her jaw quickly followed suit by dropping as well. The action caused a double-take from the entire group.

"Hi everyone!" Reva said, attempting lightness.

Ben, enjoying the moment, barreled toward them and hugged her. "Hi you." He slipped a hand from her back to reach toward Todd, who took it briefly. "Ben, Reva's brother," he said.

"Ah, the artist...I'm Todd, and this is my son, Eric."

"They're my neighbors," Reva answered before any assumptions were made.

Ben grinned. "I thought all your neighbors were old farts and married couples." He released her from the bear hug and stepped toward Todd. "You're not married, are you?"

Reva slapped him on the back of the head. "Leave him alone, goofball."

Ben's head bobbled and he growled back a nice Spanish expletive. "So, how'd you meet Reva? Don't tell me you were peeking over the fence."

Ugh. This was a mistake.

Todd kept a serious face and answered, "Datemydad.com. Haven't you heard of it? Great website."

Did he really say that? Ben's face washed with confusion. She knew he hadn't decided whether Todd was serious. Reva suppressed a giggle and confirmed. "That's right. Great website. Amazing how many single dads are out there. And you know what they say about single dads, don't you? Eric, come meet my parents' dog, Scooter." She took Eric's hand and hustled him across the yard where the dog chewed vigorously on a rawhide bone. She had severely underestimated her family's reception of her companions.

Within seconds, Maria beelined toward her. She tugged on Reva's forearm and whispered into her ear, "Where'd you find the hunk?"

"Online dating site," she said, straight-faced. She might as well keep rolling with the fun.

"No joke? Which one?"

Hook, line, and sinker. Reva kept her head down, concentrated on Eric to suppress the twitch of her mouth.

"Desperategeeks.com," she managed to say with a straight face. "Strictly for technology professionals like me."

"Wow. That sounds so incredibly thrilling." Maria rolled eyes and patted her hand to her mouth in a fake yawn. "I bet you have all kinds of things to talk about. Why didn't you mention him this morning?"

Reva flinched as a hand grasped her shoulder. "Because we were afraid we wouldn't finish getting her furniture moved in before we came over." Todd's voice sounded serious behind her yet she could feel the hint of amusement as he squeezed her flesh. His breath tickled the back of her neck. He enjoyed the charade.

"What!" Maria squealed. "You're moving in with him? Oh my God, does Mom know?" She threw a hand over her mouth and glanced nervously at their parents. Good grief, when did her sister get so gullible?

"No." Reva grinned. "And don't tell them."

"Don't tell them? Are you crazy! You know they'll have a cow. You said you're not even seeing anyone and now, all of a sudden, you're moving in with some guy and his kid? After everything you've been through!" Maria strode frantically toward the group gathered by the grill to spread the news.

Reva tsked under her breath. *And she's supposed to be the peacekeeper in the family.* Ben had already preceded her so Reva felt sure they'd have a lot to talk about for a while. It takes time to determine how to extricate a crazy sister or offspring from the clutches of yet another wrongly-suited man.

Eric looked up. "She's moving in with us, Dad?"

Todd patted him on the back. "No, buddy. It's just a joke. Nobody's moving anywhere. We're just pretending."

A twinkle passed over Eric's youthful eyes. "I love jokes! Can I pretend too?"

"Don't you think this is getting out of hand?" Reva asked.

Todd shrugged and bent to scruff the dog's ears at eye level. "It's just a little fun. Serves them right for prying. Besides, we're not hurting anyone, are we?"

He turned his face up to hers and grinned. Why'd the guy have to be so ridiculously delicious-looking?

"But I can't have them thinking I'm moving in with someone who—"

"You met on the internet? Or has a kid?" Scooter, the traitor dog, lifted and lashed out a tongue to swipe Todd's cheek. Todd didn't even back away or scrunch his face up, although he did close his mouth.

"That I barely know," Reva finished. "I've never been that careless."

Todd laughed. "Even more funny. Do they really think you're that stupid?"

It's complicated.

He leaned to a knee and looked past Reva's hip. Over her

shoulder, she noticed her parents headed their way. By the decisiveness of their steps, she expected a confrontation. "Guess the game's over, roomie," Todd said.

Clearly he had no intention of continuing the charade with her parents. It was one thing to fool her siblings—they spent too much time nosing in her private life anyway. If he thought she was going to lie to her parents about him just for fun, he was shit-out-of-luck. Reva knew better than to cross her mother. The woman had a temper that was unrivaled; even Reva's dad knew when to back down against Angelina Zamora. Reva braced herself for the explosion as she looked at the red puffy cheeks and blazing eyes on the otherwise beautiful face.

"Reva Zamora, you better not..." Her voice pitched as she raised a finger and punched it toward Reva's face. Todd stood, left Eric, and quickly strode to intercept.

"Hello, Mrs. Zamora." He held a hand out daring her not to take it. "I'm Reva's neighbor Todd, and that is my son, Eric. We met her a few days ago and she very kindly invited us over today when we were out working in the yard. I hope you don't mind us crashing your family get-together."

Angelina's mouth dropped open as she choked back any further chastising of her daughter. "But Ben said you...I mean, Maria thought..."

Reva chuckled at the way she quickly deflated.

"We were just playing around." Todd ran his fingers through his hair.

Reva's parents stared at them with cautious curiosity. They seemed unwilling to let him off the hook so quickly.

"Besides, from what little I know about your daughter, I doubt she's the rebellious type that would do something crazy. Especially without your knowledge or approval."

Right on cue, Reva's brother, Tim arrived behind her Dad. His height spanned an extra three inches over her father's round frame, which added serious intimidation to his words. "Do I need to kick some ass here?" Tim asked.

José Zamora prided himself in the fact that his sons were almost as protective of their sisters as he was. When Tim's chest bumped protectively against his back, he turned and pressed a calming hand to the chest that certainly could do some damage. "Easy there, big boy. If there's an ass-kicking required, I'll be the one to do it. Why don't you take Todd, here, over and get him and his kid a burger?"

"Dad, this isn't the divide and conquer trick is it?" Reva asked. She settled her hands on her hips in a mocked warning. "Take it easy on the guy, will you? I just met him a couple days ago. It would be embarrassing if you get him arrested before we even know anything about him."

Todd shot his head up and looked at the group. Oh, yeah. She should have remembered that José was prone to overreaction when it came to his daughters. She hated the idea of a guy being involved in a Spanish inquisition with her family, which is why she had hesitated to introduce Nick until they had dated a few months. Nick was straight-laced and conservative. Stiff, if she wanted to be honest. They were merciless with him, teasing and pranking until he was completely confused. Still, when the chips were down and Nick slapped her around for the third time, the police showed up at her doorstep and cuffed him, courtesy of one really pissed off José Zamora. And she'd been thankful.

José didn't hesitate to get involved if his daughter's safety was at stake. He likely would have gathered up Tim and Ben and whipped the guy into unconsciousness if they'd lived closer. As it was, all he had done was pick up the phone. Reva knew it tore her dad up that he had to call the cops when he preferred to teach a lesson himself. It wasn't that he was a violent man but he had been miles away and could only depend on strangers to keep her safe. It had always been his knowledge that family is a better bet every day. Fortunately, the distance kept things relatively civil and the police handled it well. Not that abuse is ever civil. As soon as Nick was in jail, Reva packed up and drove home. Her hasty departure left her with a black mark on her credit and her job history that had been difficult to erase, but no matter. She was alive, recovering, and strong. Where Nick had tried to make her feel less than capable, her family did just the opposite.

José laughed nervously about the arresting remark and clamped a hand on Todd's shoulder. "Don't worry. She's just messing around. I only sent one of her boyfriends to jail and he deserved it. Go ahead, get some food." Her dad gave a quick squeeze and released Todd to Tim.

Reva watched the two equally gorgeous men saunter toward the grill. It occurred to her that Tim would find a tough match in Todd Grisham—probably tougher than expected. Yet, Todd didn't seem the type to seek out an altercation.

"He treats you good?" José asked.

"Jesus, I barely know the guy, Dad. And if you guys keep this up, it's unlikely I'll know him for long. He's just my neighbor. He doesn't treat me any way at all. Don't go all over-protective on me, okay?"

"Can't help it. You have a history."

"History. One guy is a history?"

"Yeah, if you nearly married him, it is."

"Dad, you know I never would have married Nick. I'm too much like Mom to let some idiot with a superiority complex try to control me."

She attempted humor but it was lost. Two seconds of silence grew into ten as both accepted the undertone of what could have happened. Hindsight made it sound easy to walk away but they all knew it had taken a lot out of her. They saw the dampness in her spirit that had occurred and the wariness she tried to conceal.

"You're not at all like your mother. If you were, it never would have gone that far. You're as much my daughter as if you stepped out of my skin. There's not a person on this planet that you wouldn't try to please and win over. You always were one to attempt to befriend rather than get in a pissing match." José patted his baby girl on the cheek and followed Tim and Todd, but not before adding, "That's a good thing in most situations. You just have to know when it's not and give it up."

A roar of laughter erupted as Todd confessed to Ben and Maria. He'd punked them, a feat not easily done in her family, and they respected that. Several glances her way assured her that they should have known she couldn't snag a guy like him anyway.

CHAPTER FIVE

—— ——

Wᴴᵉⁿ the sun receded below the roof of the house, Todd met Reva's gaze. Those eyes could captivate him, big and brown, almost like velvet. Eric's head was bobbling as he fought off the sleep that threatened to end his playtime with new-found friends.

Reva passed a hand softly across his scalp and nodded. "Time to go, big guy," her voice cajoled. The kind of voice that one could get used to. The gentleness of her hand on Eric's head made Todd curious. Would she have that same gentleness if they were on his own skin? Running up his back or clutching into his pecks? The breeze caught a paper napkin on the picnic table. It floated in the air briefly before hitting the ground.

"That's right. Time to go before someone falls asleep." Todd scooped Eric into a fireman's hold with the small, dirt-covered face buried into his neck. "You don't mind leaving this early?"

"I'm thrilled. There's only so much family abuse a person can take." Reva mustered a smile.

Damn, that's a good smile even when she's tired.

"I'll make excuses while you go put him in the car. Be right there."

Todd waved at her family and carried Eric off. When she joined him a few minutes later, the smile was still there. He felt a tug at his heart. Odd, he hadn't expected to be that comfortable around Reva. Hadn't expected comfort around any woman. His marriage had tainted him, he guessed.

"That was fun," he stated when they reached her house.

Eric had dropped into a slumber in the back seat, one leg curled under him, the other slanted toward the floorboard. Todd rushed to get Reva's door before she opened it, and walked her to the step.

"I'm sorry they reacted like they did. It was unexpected. They've never really been wary of anyone I've brought home before. I guess it's different now that I—" She cut off the sentence and glanced away.

"Yeah, they told me about that." Maria had filled him in on the angry fiancé that nearly beat the shit out of her before she had the sense to pick up and leave. He wanted to kick himself for teasing her about living so close to family. Had she lived closer then, the asshole probably wouldn't have touched her. Knowing the Zamora men, they would have given him something to remember about mistreating women.

"They did? Oh *great*. Now, you'll think me a total screw-up."

"Not even close. Why would you say that?" Todd shook his head. Something stirred in him. A protective instinct perhaps? The wind caught the ruffled neckline of her shirt and blew it away from her skin. When the streetlight cast a blue glow across the curve of her breast, he recognized the instinct as nothing protective. It was more primal than that. He had enjoyed the game with her family, getting them all riled up. The mischievous sparkle in her face lit him up too. Even more interesting was his reaction to the banter. A temporary partnership had formed between them based on humor. He wondered if that had been missing for her as much as for him these past years. He liked the spark of it, the ease that she went with him in the teasing. It was alluring. The light on her face at the moment was even more so, trickling across the fullness of her lips to taunt him. Those lips probably tasted as great as they looked. It would be a damn shame if they didn't.

Huh. Guess he's finally over the bitter divorce. "I'd better go," he said. "Thanks for the invite."

"Thanks for accepting." She leveled those velvet brown eyes on him and he swallowed the lump in his throat. He was

going to kiss her. Yeah. Had to. That mouth is just sooo...
"Goodnight, Todd." She slipped inside the door and left him
standing wondering if he'd misread the signals.

The following day Annie showed up just after lunch and
whisked Eric off as if she'd missed him. Todd knew better but
thankfully Eric didn't. It was a relief that the boss didn't come
with her; Todd might have mishandled that. He knew it would
happen eventually but until now, he had considered a quick jab
to the nose would be the proper introduction. Perhaps a hand-
shake and a few choice words would work nicely too. After all,
the son-of-a-bitch saved him from the cold-hearted cow. Now,
he just needed a way to salvage Eric from her claws too. He
knew that impossible but it was still nice to dream.

The house always seemed eerily quiet after Eric left. It
usually took a while to adjust. Todd pulled the fridge open,
extracted a beer, and went to the backyard. He settled into a
lawn chair and sipped from the bottle. Was it possible that
Reva was sunbathing again this afternoon? He imagined the
black, shiny fabric of her bikini on the other side of his fence.
He pondered taking a peek through the boards, then chastised
himself. Surely, he hadn't stooped to that extent.

Another sip of beer. His cell phone chimed and he glanced
at the display. Crap. "What's up, Annie?"

"Eric's missing his tennis shoes. He said he left them at
Reva's. Who's Reva?"

None of your damn business.

"Oh, yeah. He fell asleep and I forgot to pick them up
before we left. I'll ask her about them." A convenient excuse to
talk to Reva again. He made a mental note to thank Eric.

"He needs them for school. Can you drop them by later?"
Todd half-considered telling her to come get them herself. He
didn't have time to go chasing around after her kid's things. Of
course, that was a lie. He had all the time in the world for Eric,
just not for her. Getting another brief moment with Reva was
enticing too.

"Yeah, sure." He hung up and took another swig from the
bottle. Damn, he's slipping. He should have gotten Reva's
phone number before he left. It hadn't occurred to him. She
popped in the door so fast he didn't have much time to think of

anything except the tinge of disappointment when he was left standing on the steps. He tossed the bottle into the trash and headed to the sidewalk. Hopefully, she was home this afternoon and if luck was on his side, she really *was* in that bikini again.

When she answered the door, he shelved the bikini thought. This was better. A simple pink T-shirt and jeans shorts. Her hair was pulled up high on the back of her head and her feet were bare. Damn cute.

"Well, hello there. Got tired of surfing for dates at datemydad?" she teased, leaning against the doorframe.

He laughed. *Love the cheerfulness and sense of humor.* He wondered if she knew how sexy her smile was. It could drive a man to do stupid things. "I left Eric's shoes at your parents' and his mother called for them."

"Ask and you shall receive." She pulled her hand from behind the door and handed two small size four-and-a-half scuffed shoes at him. "Mom dropped them by on her way to mass this morning. I think she wanted to check and make sure we really were kidding. She sniffed around the house like a bloodhound."

"Damn. Wish I'd come over earlier and given her something to boil about, just for grins, of course."

"She probably would have beaten you with a broom or something."

"It might have been worth it." Todd wished he could stop grinning. It felt ridiculous. "You look great by the way." *Yeah, even more ridiculous. God, this sucks – completely awkward.* It had been ages since he'd even cast a second glance at a woman without suspicion. None of that now. No. More like amusement and as much as he hated to admit it, desire.

She swiped a hand over her hair. "Thanks. You have a cell phone?"

He nodded and pulled it from his pocket to show her. She took it, fumbled around a bit, and then handed it back. "There. If you think of anything else he forgot or need to retrieve the rodent, you can call me next time and save a trip around the block."

He stared at the phone display. Aw, she gave him her

number. He didn't even have to ask. She had been thinking about him too. He doubted those thoughts were as hot and heavy.

"No problem." He slipped the phone back in his pocket and turned to leave, lifting the shoes in a wave. "Thanks for these."

"You're becoming quite the nuisance, you know." The sparkle in her voice softened the words. He circled around.

"You know you missed me." He tried to remember how he acted in this kind of situation but nothing came. *Screw it. Playfulness is sexy, right?*

"Yeah, you caught me—that's the feeling. It's disguised as annoyance."

Okay, sort of sexy. Or not.

"That feeling in your gut isn't annoyance, Reva, it's lust." Oh shit, did he really say that crap?

"Wow. Does that line work for you?" She raised an eyebrow and dropped a hand to her hip. The slight lift of the T-shirt bared some bronzed skin.

Yikes, he had it backward. The lust appeared to emanate from him, not her. "Never used it before," he answered.

"Word of warning – don't. Most women run like hell from that kind of talk. Besides, you don't seem the type to need to say it." *That was a compliment, right?*

"I've never made a woman run. Stomp out in a tantrum, scream a little, or just stop caring, yes, but not run. The question is, do you?" *Yeah, smooth. Real smooth. What a dumb thing to say.* He decided to walk away before it got worse.

"Do I what—care?"

He shook his head. "Run like hell." His hands shook a bit, reminding him he was in uncharted waters, and probably needed a life boat or something. Flirting never had been his best skill.

"Oh." She tilted her head to the side and he almost saw the dimples come out. "Maybe. I'll have to think about that a while."

"You do that. But don't get all worried. I'm not really the type to chase." He held up the shoes. "Better get these back to Eric. He'll need them tomorrow." He took a few steps backward and tried to give her his best smile, whatever that was. Unfortunately it was overshadowed by the fact that his calf slammed against the bumper of her car. Reva erupted in a full dimple laugh and threw back the cute little ponytail.

"Stick to humor rather than the lines, Todd. It works for you."

Okay, so he still had a bit of the old spark in him. That was good to know. Annie attempted to kill that part but she hadn't succeeded. He was okay with humor. That could grow into something, couldn't it? Huh. Did he really want it to? He raised his shoulders, and jogged back around the block before he did something else really stupid.

Avoidance was a great tactic when it came to pain and ugliness. He dropped the shoes at Annie's door and high-tailed it out without even knocking. Normally he'd go in and talk to Eric. He suffered through Annie's complaints and criticism as a trade-off for a few minutes with the kid. Not tonight. Nothing was going to burst this bubble – he'd enjoyed the time with Reva. When he was back home, he sent a quick text telling Annie where to find the shoes.

CHAPTER SIX

——— ———

Tuesday morning came a lot sooner than Reva wanted. With little progress on Adam's project, she knew it was time for that discussion. Still, after hearing Adam unload on Gavin last week, she questioned the possibility of a positive outcome. *No worries, girl. This is what you do best. You love helping people overcome obstacles and succeed.*

She peeked into Adam's office mid-morning and mustered her best cheerful look. "Can you stop by so we can discuss the status of your migration project?"

He stared right through her without even a twitch. "Yes, ma'am."

Reva hung around her office until lunch, finishing up paperwork, signing off on invoices and updating her monthly status report for the board. Adam never showed. He knew her afternoon was filled with back to back meetings and it annoyed her that he intentionally dissed the request.

She opened her office door at 4:30 and dropped her keys and notebook on the desk, before pressing a button on the phone to check messages. There were fourteen waiting. She heaved a sigh and dropped into the chair to work through each one. Reva always jotted the message details on a legal pad along with date and time, and then called back the people individually. Four of the calls were questions about Adam's project. Apparently he'd told a few people it would go live Friday! The project hadn't even reached the first phase of a four-stage deployment. No wonder the callers were panicked. In the middle of the ninth message, three taps reverberated on her door.

Forcing a smile, Reva lifted her head to answer. She half-expected another annoyed staff member to confront her about the timeline and what they should do.

"You wanted to talk to me?" Adam said. She glanced at the clock. A quarter to five. Yeah, he really took her request seriously.

"That's right. I did earlier today but you've waited too long and I'm leaving shortly. What's this I hear about your migration going live this weekend? We haven't even looked at it yet, nor have we done any deployment tests or functionality tests. Surely it's not that far along?"

"All we have to do is set up the users in the software and send out the instructions. They're smart—they should have no problem doing this."

She swallowed the verbal venting she wanted to release. "Have you tested the migration yet on our test server with some of the machines?"

"I ran it on mine but not on the test server. It went fine."

"Your machine isn't the server and doesn't have any live files to port over. You're also running at higher permissions than most users, so it wouldn't be possible to validate that staff won't run into either permission or server/connectivity related issues. Also, if my memory serves me right, when I did the last one three years ago, there was a script that had to run for each user on the local machine in order to get their environment set up correctly."

"It worked fine for me. I tested the script—no problems. Why are you making such a big deal out of it?"

"Adam, we should have talked about this a week ago and certainly way before we start informing staff. I'm sorry but there's no way we can start this weekend. Not without testing everything on standard user accounts. You're an admin, that doesn't count."

Adam glared at Reva. He stood over her desk with clenched fists. "Don't you think that's overkill for such a small project?"

She sensed the tension in his voice and it startled her.

Glancing up, she thought he might lunge at her. Reva rose quickly and did her best to diffuse the situation by softening the tone of her voice and motioning to the chair in front of her desk. "Why don't you sit down, Adam, and we'll figure out what needs to happen and set a schedule to it."

He looked at the office door, she thought to check for anyone passing, and then lowered into the chair. "I don't need your help. I can do this."

"I'm sure you can, but this isn't a small project. We're migrating software that all 3000 users will need access to. We have to test every scenario, even remote access, and we can't do that without a project plan and detailed schedule that includes testing every part. Until we have that, we're not going forward, and I certainly don't expect you to do this alone, it's too big. Who do you want to help you? We'll meet with them tomorrow to discuss it. I'm sorry but you're just not ready yet and we're not going to fly by the seat of our pants on this one. Does that make sense?"

"Very. Is there anything else you want from me?"

Super. He didn't like that at all. How else was she supposed to tell him? The guy's a grown man, not a two-year old.

"Not that I can think of at the moment." She hesitated. "Oh wait, I did mention at the staff meeting last week that everyone needs to start putting together their goals for next year. We'll incorporate that into the individual performance reviews as well as our strategic plan. So, once we get the project back in scope, you might want to give some thought to that."

It comforted her to see him appear calmer. Reva smiled encouragement. "Have a good evening, Adam. Thanks for meeting with me."

The time on the clock said five-thirty. All the other staff members were gone for the day. Did he actually mutter "whatever" as he stepped to the door?

"One last thing, though." She probably should wait until her temper calmed but she went ahead when he met her eyes. "Next time I ask you to stop by, don't wait so long, okay?"

"I was busy."

This was getting really *old*. She took a labored breath. It required a good amount of control to bite back a response.

"I'm sure you were. I'll be more specific in the future, if that helps. The longer we put off these discussions the more the project stretches out. Let's keep an eye on how this reflects on the department and work together to get it finished."

Not to mention the only reason you delayed was to piss me off. Reva felt exhaustion working into her shoulder blades. She pulled her purse and laptop bag from the desk and walked him to the door. The door clicked closed behind her as she said, "See you tomorrow."

Adam ignored her words and strode away.

Hmmm. That didn't go as she hoped and, for the life of her, she wasn't sure if he was better or worse for the discussion. How could she have handled it differently? Tomorrow's meeting with the additional staff involved should go much better. In all honesty, if this had happened pre-Nick she would have lost her temper and got in his face. After spending a year evading confrontations that escalated beyond the yelled exchanges, she had a different perspective on how to read emotions. It had been a rude awakening to be a victim of anything, let alone an abusive boyfriend. An awakening that battered bruises into her arms and back, then left her with a realization that all people absolutely *do not* react like her family does. For all their big words, loud voices, and sassiness – her parents had never laid a punishing hand on any of their kids. They didn't need to. When anyone was dangerously out of line, the entire family knew and got involved. Family amusement was a very influential method of behavior correction. If that didn't work, they counseled. Over and over again.

Reva sighed as she sat watching the evening news in the kitchen. She scraped her fork through the sauce on a plate of warmed tacos with disinterest. Her world had changed irreversibly in the past few years. So had she. Every facial expression, every flinch, every tone change in a voice worried her. She chastised herself on a daily basis for taking things too seriously. Nick was a random anomaly. Normal people don't act like that, so her Dad advised. Still, she had vowed when she moved back home that she would never get in a similar situation again. For some reason, Adam scared her. She knew she was likely being paranoid, but still...something about him made the hairs on the back of her neck stand at attention. Realistically, he probably hadn't intended to lunge at her. She very likely overreacted to his gestures and expressions. Unfortunately, as much as a person wanted to dispense of their past, it was impossible to do so. If she could wipe the time with Nick from her mind and soul, she would have already done so. She hated that her old, avant-guard attitude had been replaced with this....whatever it was. She didn't even know herself now.

Todd Grisham had seen past it though. He had teased and welcomed her in a most comfortable way. There had been no threat or concern in his words or touch.

Her cell buzzed and broke the trance. She didn't recognize the number and considered letting it go to voicemail. After three rings, she answered.

Todd. He had a seductively kind voice on the phone. Or in person for that matter. She pictured his smile.

"I'm going over to sign up for the softball team and thought I'd ask if you wanted to sign up too. I can put your name on the list if you do."

"I forgot about that. Uh, okay. Tell you what—meet me at the corner and I'll walk along, if that's okay." Excellent. That would take her mind off silly things like abusive ex's and ominous employees. She wasn't all that big on softball but what the hell. Maybe it would ease the drama. Surely pounding the hell out of a leather ball would be a good outlet?

Todd slowed to a stop at the corner Reva mentioned, which segmented her street from the community park. The park spanned five blocks and had a walking path around it with a duck pond opposite the pool, and a lone baseball diamond nestled in the bosom. Her house was the third door away and he imagined she could hear the park noises on a still day. A nice-sized Texas pecan tree graced the corner and he rested a shoulder against it as he waited on her approach. The breeze glancing along his temple predicted a reasonably cool evening for spring. It also funneled the scent of ligustrum toward him, a scent that either made one smile or sneeze...depending on the tendency toward allergies to plant life. Todd smiled and twitched his nose.

Reva's dimples were in full force as she bounced toward him in a gray T-shirt and navy shorts. Her ponytail wagged in rhythm to her steps, a few tendrils slipping out in wisps across her face. She always looked so—clean. She also normally appeared outwardly happy but in the short time they'd spent together, he noticed a rumbling unease hidden behind the smiles. It occurred to him the warmth never seemed to completely sink into her eyes. She had great dimples and a ready smile, but something more lurked in the background and it made him curious.

"Thanks," she said.

"What for?"

"Getting me out. Today was a rough day. I needed out."

It wasn't his nature to pry. Annie had hated that about him. Whenever she was upset about something, she had expected him to pick and prod information from her until she spouted her feelings like a fountain. She liked the attention. He had thought it a stupid game. If a person wanted someone to understand them, they should just say what they meant. No need for pretenses.

"Sorry to hear that but on a night like this, you can't bring your work home. It's too perfect." He raised a hand at the sky, noting that the sun was blinking its last bit of light on the horizon. "We'd better hurry before it's too dark to see." He fell in beside her and picked up the pace.

"Feel like running?" Reva asked.

"Running or jogging?"

"Whatever you want. I think I could beat you." She moved in a mock trot and glanced back at him.

"Only if you take the head-start you're working on right now, cheater."

She laughed. "Okay, count to three then."

He recognized the challenge in her eyes. He'd seen her jogging in the neighborhood so he knew she was confident he'd never keep up. Obviously, she didn't pay as much attention as he did.

"One, two, three, go." He took off in a sprint after giving a quick wink that caught her off guard.

"Hey! I wasn't ready."

She gained on him in two seconds. He expected her to pass but she didn't, she fell into step beside him and matched step for step. A loud shout in front of them caught their attention. They swerved their heads just in time to see the softball barreling toward them from one of the yards. A young girl lunged after it in white baseball pants with stained knees. Reva ducked and the ball caught Todd hard on the forehead. Wham! He was blinded for a second as it bounced off his hard skull and landed in the crook of a nearby tree. He staggered to catch his footing.

"Now, look what you've done, mister!" The little girl glared at him with hands on hips. Her frown threatened to permanently wrinkle her feminine face. She threw a hand up to point at the tree. "How am I supposed to get that down from there?"

She didn't even ask if he was okay. She certainly didn't notice the beginning of a goose egg on his forehead, nor did she see the water forming in his eyelids. Tough little turd.

"You're the one that bounced it off my head, kiddo. How was I supposed to control where it went from there when I didn't know it was coming?" He rubbed his temple.

The girl picked the cap off her head and turned it backward, placing it over the loose braids. "Technically, *he* bounced it off your head." She pointed to a boy standing in the yard with eyes averted. "If he threw better, I could have caught it but he stinks at baseball. Still, it's better than nothin so...you're gonna have to get the ball down. My parents won't let me climb trees anymore, since I fell and broke my arm last summer. That's the only ball we have." She crossed her arms over her chest and waited.

Todd blinked twice to focus and peered up at the ball nestled perfectly in the crook of two tree branches about eight feet up. He stepped to the tree, raised a hand and reached. The blurriness sent his hand into the bark first. Once he regrouped, he stabbed at the ball. *Plunk.* It disappeared into the tree. *Crap.* There was a hole in the trunk.

"You're kidding me." The little girl huffed and wagged her head back and forth. Todd pitied the little boy.

"Whoa. Don't worry, I'll get it," he assured. He stood on his toes and bent an arm into the crevice, feeling around for leather. No luck. He strained further, patting again in the opening with no success. "I'm sorry, I can't reach it. Do you have a ladder?"

Reva chuckled. "Let me help. Lift me up and I'll get it. My arm's smaller—I can probably reach better."

"You really want to put your arm down there? Who knows why that hole's there. Might be something in it." He eyed her.

"Yeah, an arm-eating, killer softball," Reva teased. She motioned for him to come closer and lifted a leg. "Come on, lift me up."

"Okay, but don't blame me if you come out with more than just the ball. Say a bite mark or two," he cautioned.

"You're really not building confidence, you know. I was perfectly ready to do this until you said *that*."

Todd grasped her foot with both hands and balanced it against his knee. He gave her a boost that sent her up into the air. She leaned against him, her butt balanced on his shoulder. He could smell her lotion, a nice earthy scent. She shifted and without warning, he had a butt cheek flattened against his eye, blocking the view. She leaned into the tree, floundering for the ball.

"Uh, Reva?"

"I just need to..." she grumbled, "get farther. There. Almost have it. Just a little more. Give me a push."

He guessed she didn't know her ass was plastered to his face. The little girl and boy had moved away and tried hard to contain their giggles. When the boy started to speak, the girl punched him in the arm and shushed him.

"Reva," Todd said.

"Just a little more. Come on. I can feel it at the end of my fingers." Her toes dug into his palm.

"Reva! I can barely hold you. If you keep shoving your behind in my face, I'll drop you. If you can't get it, I'll buy them another ball." *Awkward.*

"Oh, God. I'm sorry." She tried to pull up. "Oh. No."

"Now what?" Todd asked.

"I'm stuck....my arm is stuck."

He squinted through the one eye that wasn't blocked by her hip. Her torso was completely invisible. "You're kidding."

"No. Not kidding. Why would I kid about that? I'm stuck!"

"Well, get unstuck before I drop you," Todd answered.

He staggered for a second as she dug a foot into his stomach and tried to move. The two kids laughed outright, clutching their stomachs with gloved hands. "Hey!" He scowled at them. They sobered instantly. "Go get some soap or some oil or something. We need to lubricate her arm and see if we can pull it out." He motioned with his head toward their front door.

"Yes sir." The two disappeared inside, returning with their parents and a younger brother in tow. The mother had a box filled with things. Dish Soap, bar soap, bath oil, Crisco, butter and yum – whip cream? What kind of family is this? He crooked an eye at the approaching woman.

"What do you have planned there? A greasy arm sundae with whipped cream on top?" Todd asked.

"Well, the kids told me what happened and we saw you out the window. I thought we'd start with the soap and then just work through the rest until we found something that worked." She stifled a grin as she looked at Reva's butt smashed against the side of his head. "Are you okay up there, honey?" the woman asked.

"Not really," Reva snipped. "Things could definitely be better. My arm hurts, my legs are cramping, and I have something crawling down my elbow."

That brought a snicker from both parents. Todd was amazed at her composure. She didn't freak. She didn't scream. Wow.

"I'm Carlie and this is my husband Ronnie. The baseball throw came from Ron, Junior and the mouthy one is our daughter, Reva. Don't worry, we'll get you out." Carlie glanced at Ron. "Get the ladder, babe."

Todd lifted the side of his face that was free into a smile and tried to nod. "I'm Todd and this is Reva. I would say nice to meet you but I'd rather do so under different circumstances."

Reva's muffled voice came from somewhere on the other side of her hips. "Cut the small talk, guys. Just hurry up and get me out of here! Whatever crawled down my elbow has just found a friend that's headed up toward my armpit!"

Holy Shit, you're a tough one. He tried not to chuckle. Todd could feel Reva's legs trembling. Muscle spasms, he assumed. He stroked her ankle with his thumb and she went completely limp. "Are you okay?" he asked.

No answer.

"Reva?" One, two, three seconds passed.

"Yeah, I'm good." Her voice softened and he knew she had lied.

The ladder arrived and Ron, Senior climbed it. He squeezed dish soap into the small opening below Reva's shoulder. She attempted to work her arm to distribute the liquid.

"Well?" Todd asked.

"Nope. Not working."

"Okay then," Carlie said, not to be deterred. "Try this." She handed Ron the oil. Even if it didn't work, it sure smelled good. Minutes later, they had gone through all but the whipped cream. No change, and Reva's voice weakened considerably. Todd's shoulder ached from Reva's weight. As much as he liked looking at her, this was not the angle he had hoped for. His hands were beyond numb but he knew if he let her fall, she'd likely yank her arm and cause damage.

"What do you think, Todd?" Carlie held the can up and shook it to and fro.

"Don't bother. With everything else we've poured in, there will be all sorts of insects swarming. Add that and she's sure to get stung. I doubt it'd help anyway." He raised his free eye to meet hers but she stared over his head.

"What's wrong?" Todd asked.

"Nothing. There are a few neighbors watching." The distant sound of sirens crooned in the night, gaining volume as they approached. *A few neighbors and here comes the city fire department.*

"The fire department?" Reva asked from the depths of the tree trunk. "You called the fire department? That's just great."

"No, we didn't call," Todd corrected. "Someone apparently did, but not us."

At least fifteen people stood around. They talked, giggled, pointed. Good thing she couldn't see any of this. He felt her legs tremble.

The sirens and flashing lights pulled to the curb, the crowd broke to allow access. Todd was pushed aside as a burly fireman took his place. *Thank God.* Thirty minutes later, Reva was freed from the tree with a bruised and well-oiled arm...covered in...ants. The tree had sustained worse damage. It had a gaping hole where one limb had been removed.

When Reva's head surfaced for the first time since the incident started, the crowd broke into cheers and clapped. A wolf-whistle came too, and her face changed from sheet-white to crimson in seconds. Only her eyes betrayed the fear that she suppressed. She didn't cry. She didn't scream. She didn't yell. She didn't move. Still there was pure terror in her expression. *Was that fabricated stillness her coping mechanism?* Todd realized he had sorely underestimated the level of abuse she had survived. Until tonight, he had hoped to spend more time with Reva. Now, that seemed tinged with potential drama. Drama wasn't something he normally endured. Not anymore.

Reva snapped out of her trance and readjusted the ponytail in her hair to remove the entwined bark. "You are sooo buying me dinner and a beer or two."

Todd relaxed and smiled. There was hope. Yay. Atta girl. "That's sooo not a problem. Let's go. We'll make quite a pair—me with a knot on my head, and you with scratches all over your arm."

"Been there done that. The hard way." She shrugged. "This should be a cakewalk."

He didn't dare push for details.

CHAPTER SEVEN

Celebrity Status achieved through humiliation leads to exhaustion. Reva's front door took a beating over the next few days from the barrage of neighbors checking in. She assumed it was more for amusement than concern over her well-being. Regardless, in quick time she had learned every detail about the people that surrounded her. Plus it had served to lessen her panic at the sound of a door knock.

Her concerns at work paled compared to the stories that traversed the neighborhood. She much preferred her pre-existing blindness to the many flaws and drama that had previously escaped her attention. Knowledge, in this case, was definitely *not* power, but rather another mechanism to increase her fear and agitation. For the community, it appeared to be a source of pride to share a tidbit of information on a neighbor that had not yet been heard. Her story was obviously the biggest excitement since Bradley Harris on West Sycamore was arrested for growing marijuana in his attic. There was a little humor in that story as well. Who guessed that old bald guy had it in him?

When a knock on the door occurred Thursday night simultaneous to her cell phone ringing, Reva practically jumped out of her skin. Temptation to ignore the door and the curious neighbor crowding it surfaced as she glanced at the phone display. She still checked every time before answering to make sure it wasn't Nick calling. There had been no reason to suspect he wanted to but she couldn't suppress the learned reaction even though months had passed. She recognized her sister's number. She had a dilemma; ignoring the door would tell the person standing outside it she was in when the cell stopped ringing. Ignoring the cell would allow her to bypass both and, at the moment, that certainly was appealing.

She answered it at the same time she unlocked the door. "Have I caught you doing anything illegal?" Maria asked. She really needed a new greeting. Reva jerked the door open and grinned. Todd.

"Do thoughts count?" she answered.

"Huh?" Todd asked. When Reva pointed to the phone and mouthed her sister's name, he nodded. "You ready for practice?" he said.

"Reva?" Maria's voice echoed. "You have someone there? Please don't tell me it's that guy you brought to Mom and Dad's—and he better not be moved in."

Reva giggled. "Yep, it's him and no he's not, but don't rule it out yet. I'd do just about anything to get Mom and Dad out of my hair. I'm on my way out, Mar. Can I call you in a couple hours?"

Maria reluctantly let her go and it pleased Reva that her curiosity had been aroused.

She dropped the phone in her sports bag, zipped it closed, and stepped out to lock the door. It had been nice of him to stop by and get her. It's really odd the things that bother a person when they've dealt with an abusive relationship. For those small few that had already passed beyond the potential of danger and experienced what came next, the possibility of walking alone at night might have been unthinkable. It definitely was her least attractive mode of travel or entertainment. She rarely ventured out just to walk, and certainly not alone. Running felt safer. Being out alone had become a vulnerability in her past life; one that she had no intention of repeating. That had been placed firmly behind and this was the time to start refreshed, confident, and as Neil Armstrong said on the moon, *go boldly forth where no man has gone before.* Okay, maybe a lot of people have been in this situation before. Still, they weren't living her life at the moment, which substantiated the reasoning that she had no intention of being stupid. Been there, done that. Not going back.

As Reva and Todd walked leisurely to the ball diamond, they spoke casually, making idle conversation. The slow pace tortured her. *Can this man not walk any faster? Does he always meander through life as if nothing matters?*

"We're twenty minutes early, you know," he said.

She forced herself to release the fist that she'd clenched her right hand into.

"We'll be the first ones to show up so you don't need to rush."

"Sorry, it's habit. I always walk fast."

"And you run. Or at least when I see you, you're running somewhere."

She ran in the mornings, and made sure to watch every movement around her when she did. He had already mentioned seeing her. She wondered if he'd noticed her other habits. Like that she always crossed the street when someone was in their yard or approaching her on the sidewalk. She even did so when a car drove toward her sluggishly.

"Would you prefer to run now?"

"Actually, no. I'm sorry. I'll slow down." She hesitated to explain. It could be an instant conversation killer to do so. Besides, apparently her family had already said something. No need to dwell on it. *Go forth.*

The softball practice was a nice tension reliever, and it proved a pleasant surprise to discover she hadn't lost her skills. The team was made up of a great deal of young parents or newlyweds. Only one other single person attended, a young man named Rod. "As in Stewart" he had told them when introduced. Reva guessed his mother had been a fan. Rod took an instant liking to Reva and didn't attempt to conceal it. Apparently, he had signed up at the request of his brother and wife, who felt it would help him to meet people. Rod had moved nearby less than three months before.

"I knew you'd nail this." Todd smiled when he returned from rounding the bases after his ground hit made it past two fielders.

"What are you talking about? You're the one that just hit the snot out of the ball."

"Errors. I made it around on errors, not on the hit, but I'll take it any way I can."

After practice, the group lounged in the dugout around a cooler filled with drinks. Idle conversation about kids, friends, parents, and the home owner's association seemed to be the main topics. Reva contributed little as she took a random swig of beer. Though quiet, it had been a welcome feeling to be outside with a group, almost relaxing. When she gathered her things and headed home, Todd fell into step beside her, and she was glad for it.

"You seemed a bit distracted earlier. Everything okay?"

He had no idea. He was just being polite and she certainly didn't intend to dump her baggage on him.

"Work is... Work. I have a small co-worker issue but it'll resolve itself in a few days." She had been confident of that last week but now that confidence had wavered. Adam's confrontational attitude, coupled with his lack of response, made her think back to her original unease. She needed to really think about the best way to proceed with him.

"Want to tell me about it?" He offered it almost as an after-thought.

She sized him up for a brief moment. "Nope. Not really."

"Okay. Maybe some other time then. You know, you're a pretty good athlete. I've seen you run and you move easily and more graceful than most. I assume you ran track and played ball in high school?"

"Does it matter? That's all over with now. I run now to stay in shape and be prepared." She realized the last word was a bad choice after it was already spoken.

"Prepared for what?" He stepped off the curb to cross the street as a car whizzed past. Reva jumped back, yanking on his arm. "Don't panic. They saw me."

"I know – but they were so close." She hesitated until the car had reached the corner and turned away before following. She picked up the pace and clipped across the street to the sidewalk, darting a glance to ensure no other pedestrians were nearby.

"Reva, stop for a minute." He still hadn't made it to the curb and she fidgeted as she waited. "You have dirt all over your back from where you dove after the ball at second. Let me dust it off."

"No." She craned her neck to see her backside and swatted a hand across her butt twice. "I've got it."

Todd's hand swiped down her hip in a pat, catching her off guard. Reva jolted and ducked.

"Hey. Hey." He lowered his voice and crooned. "You missed a spot. I'm not going to hurt you." Todd pulled his hand back to his hip and stood watching her face. Reva couldn't meet his gaze. She couldn't let him see the barely concealed panic that occurred whenever an unexpected touch happened.

"I'm sorry. I didn't mean to do that. I just – was surprised."

Another car turned toward them and slowly moved by. She watched it as it trailed along, a mother and her children on the way home from somewhere. The mother waved and smiled, and Reva returned the wave. Is it normal to peer into each car and take a mental note of the features? She'd done it for so long it was impossible to stop.

"You've become a celebrity around here," Todd mused. "The girl with her butt hanging out of the tree. Just what I always wanted to be remembered for."

Todd laughed. She liked the sound, and the way the muscles in his neck flexed when he tossed his head back. He reached for her softball glove and dropped it over the handle of the bat he carried, letting it slide to rest over his own well-worn glove.

"That's better than being the guy whose face was smashed against your ass for two hours."

She felt heat rising in her face. "About that. Can we just pretend it didn't happen? You know, not talk about it again?"

"That might be a little hard since we'll probably walk by that tree every time we go to the ball park. Not to mention the neighbors have been around checking on us all the time. Pretty nosy bunch, don't you think?"

They reached the corner by her house and she turned. Before picking up the pace to walk the last few steps alone, she smiled. "It's kind of like going to my parents."

knew it mattered that he did so. She had obviously been through a lot more than she wanted to share. If he was honest, he didn't want to know. He was not the kind of person to rescue hurt animals and nurse them back to health, and certainly not a man to rescue wounded women. Eric was like that, not him. Todd liked to think he could sympathize with those less fortunate, but he had never been very good at nurturing. Maybe because he'd had so little of it himself.

Reva had something bothering her that she was wrestling with internally. He had no desire to pry it out of her and certainly no interest in hearing about workplace gossip. Did that make him cold? As he watched the movement of her hips which still carried a spackling of dirt across the back pockets of her shorts, he knew the answer was no. There was nothing cold about the feelings he had around Reva. Just the opposite.

She turned as she put a key in her door and waved before disappearing inside. In fact, he decided to make a mission out of getting that smile to reach her eyes. He didn't want to know her drama but he certainly did want to get her past it.

The following days flew by for Todd. He found a new line of loungers that would sell well on his website and worked through the contract language, then set a delivery schedule with the supplier. A few emails back and forth to another possible vendor and he had an idea to open another branch of stores. He still marveled at how well the business had done the past few years, literally growing from a small landscape business to a conglomerate that shipped worldwide. He had done without an office for years, focusing the biggest part of efforts on the shipping, receiving, and marketing. It had all been done from a small warehouse he rented thirty minutes away. This year when he had finally expanded to more stores, he needed a space to use as a pseudo-headquarters. That didn't seem likely at the warehouse. So, he moved everything another ten minutes from the house into a larger building that consisted of three offices, a small kitchen, and a warehouse that equaled in size to the prior one. It frightened him that the business had grown so quickly.

Still, it had not taken any serious toll on him financially or health-wise. The concerns had been for the new staff he added and the longevity of their success. With gained achievement

Todd stood at the corner until Reva reached her door. He

came the realization that he had new responsibilities for the lives of his employees. Relationship-wise, it had been a relief to drown himself in work rather than consider how long it had been since he'd been out with a woman or simply "in" with a woman. When he had not been at work, his time centered on Eric—at least on the weekends that he was lucky enough to have the kid around. Since he'd met Reva, he found himself spending more time peering at the roof of her house over the fence. Sometimes he had simply sat in the backyard with a beer and considered what she was doing.

Thursday night, he stood in the kitchen and noticed Reva's light and wondered how she had managed her problem at work.

"Hey." He was tired but tried to be cheerful when she answered her cell. "How's your week been so far?"

"Fabulous." Her voice sounded otherwise. "What's up?"

"I have something for you. Mind if I bring it by? I could drop it over the fence but I know how that bothers you."

"What is it?"

He laughed. "Just wait and see. Be there in fifteen minutes."

Dusk settled over their quiet little streets as he stepped up to her door. He knocked, aware that she would look out the window and door to validate his presence before opening up. Reva didn't disappoint. Not by looking through the door as he waved, and not by being exceptionally perky and sexy in her shorts and tank top. Her hair was swept back in a tie but much of it had fallen forward to frame her face. The look was refreshing in the fact that she'd taken no time to worry over it. He smiled when she opened the door. He reached for her hand. Reva drew back briefly, then let him take it.

"Come on. It's in the yard." He nodded at the pile of rocks he'd brought over in his truck.

"Rocks? You brought me rocks? Have you been talking with Ben?" She followed him.

"No, it's not a pile of rocks. Look," he held up a clear hose, "it's a waterfall for your backyard. I thought you might like it as an addition to all the other artwork. It's from a supplier in Phoenix that wants our business. I asked him to send some samples a while back, and this is one of them. I've set up the others at our office warehouse so we can test them out. This was an extra. What do you think? I can install it for you if you like it." He watched her survey the mass of rocks and plastic. Reva trod lightly around it with her hands in the back pockets of her shorts as if to evaluate what it would look like. Todd pulled a crumpled paper from his pocket, smoothed the edges, then held it out to her.

"Here's what you can expect it to look like when finished. It requires electricity and water so I thought you might want it by the back door. If you don't think it'll work for you, I can keep it. It just seemed a good fit with all the rest of the..."

"Junk?"

"No, I wasn't going to say that." He laughed. "Artwork was more the word I had in mind." He peered at her with hands on hips. Admittedly, it would be hard to picture the end result without the paper he had handed to her. Since he'd already assembled two at the office, he knew the basic look and felt confident the end result would please her.

"Uh, okay. I can help you with it. How long does it take to assemble? This isn't going to be like my old dollhouse is it? My parents bought one of those build-it-yourself dollhouse kits when I was ten and we worked on it two or three nights a week for over a month. It sat on the counter in the den for ages unfinished because I lost interest. I basically grew out of dolls while it sat there. My dad finally admitted defeat and gave it to a little girl down the street."

"What are you trying to tell me?"

"That if it can be done quickly and efficiently so I can use it right away, I'm all in. Otherwise...count me out."

"So, you're not a very patient woman then?" he teased.

She shook her head, sending the ponytail whisking back and forth. "Nope. Not for that kind of thing. I love building things but I love *finished* things more. I do technical projects for a living so I'm pretty good at them...and I like to get them done ontime. On the other hand, I *do* believe in doing things proper and sturdy. So, I guess you could say I'm patient to a point, but once it crosses the realm into tedious and boring, you lose me."

Todd held up his hands. "You might get a little dirty doing this but I doubt it will take us more than one day, maybe only an afternoon. Depending on how much you like hard work of course."

"Is that a challenge?"

"Pretty much. What do you think?"

The rumble of a car approaching caught her interest and she glanced down the street. Todd noticed that she moved a few steps toward the house and frowned. "Okay, come by on Saturday but not in the afternoon. I don't want to be out working in the yard in the heat of the day. Be here at eight."

"Sounds good."

"You're not going to leave this here in the front yard, are you?"

Todd laughed. She sounded like his mother. "Of course not, but I wasn't going to go traipsing around in your backyard without talking to you first. Not only would that be bad manners but, based on the scare you had when Bugsy made his escape, I was afraid I'd catch you topless or something. Then you'd probably call the cops on me." His thoughts slid back to the strings left loose around her neck from her bikini and the way they'd tantalized him as if they'd fall at any moment. Maybe he *should* have gone to the backyard first anyway.

"Yeah, probably. I'll help you carry it back and we can stack it next to the door until Saturday." Reva bent over and picked up the largest of the rocks. He noticed she tested the weight before lifting to prevent injury, which indicated she had done a fair bit of lifting before. He admired that she hadn't been afraid of the work.

"Are you trying to impress me?" he asked.

"Impress you how?" She craned her neck up at him.

"By going for the biggest rock just to show you're not helpless."

"No, but if that impresses you, feel free to wonder at my incredible charm and beauty while you're at it."

Todd stacked two rocks on top of each other and hoisted them in his arms. "I already noticed that part, Reva, but it's good to know you're strong as an ox too. That'll come in handy next time I get in a gang fight and need Helga the Bonecrusher on my side. Been doing a little weightlifting along with the running?"

He followed as she worked her way to the backyard with the

rock. As much as she wanted him to think her an Amazon woman, she struggled under the weight. The thought to drop his and help was fleeting. She wouldn't want the help. She pressed the rock against the wall of her house while she maneuvered her weight under it.

"I stay in shape. You never know when you might be in a position where you have to kick some ass." She pulled the rock back and crossed the remaining distance to her back door before dropping it to the ground. The thud punctuated her statement quite effectively.

"Or protect yourself. Remind me not to piss you off," he answered before adding his rocks to her pile of one. They carried the rest of the pieces back and when done, she offered him an iced tea.

"You're bleeding, Reva." He noticed the drip trailing off the scratches on her arm. "You must have aggravated the tree scratches."

He moved toward her to get a look. Reva lifted her arm and peered at the flesh.

"It's nothing. I'll wrap it up." She swiped the blood with her finger.

Todd wrapped his fingers around her forearm and lifted it. He leaned in to get a better view of the damage. Her pulse spiked but she didn't pull away.

"I shouldn't have let you carry all this. I'm sorry," he said.

"What the ..." A booming voice said from the gate. Reva's brother Tim glanced over the fence posts, taking in Todd's hand, Reva's scratches, the words, and – the blood. "No way!" Tim bellowed as he slammed the gate open and barreled through with Ben on his heels.

"You son of a bitch," Ben added.

Todd dropped Reva's arm as the two pit-bulls charged him, their faces filled with anger.

"It's not like that guys!" Reva stepped between them to stop her brothers' attack but they pushed her aside. "He was just helping me."

"I see that. Helping you get cut up and pushed around again." Tim shoved Todd against the brick and levered a forearm against his throat, pinching off his breath.

Todd had no way to defend himself against both men. Doing so would have escalated the issue further. He simply held up his hands and faced the palms toward them. He said nothing.

"You think it's okay to take advantage of women, smartass?" Ben's voice was low and threatening behind Tim's mass. He reached in and grabbed a handful of Todd's hair. "Think again. She's been through that already and there's no way—"

Reva screamed and lunged onto Tim's back, tightening her arms around his neck and forcing him to release Todd. She pushed the fingers of one hand into his hair, pulling hard while she threaded the other hand over his eyes and blinded him. "He didn't touch me guys! He. Didn't. Touch. Me. It's just a scratch."

"Sure. You've said that before," Tim growled.

With Tim occupied, Ben stepped in and took over by landing a solid punch to Todd's face. *Damn.* Todd leaned down cupping a hand over his right eye, which very likely had started swelling. He couldn't open it. He held out a hand to try to wield off the next movement, which ended up a good swift kick to the shin. He felt lucky – it had been aimed at the groin. His fast reaction readjusted the target.

"Ouch! Jesus, this is *not* happening." Todd groaned and fell to the ground to rub his shin.

"Stop it!" Reva shouted. "Stop it! He's done *nothing. Nothing*, you hear me? He helped me carry these rocks back here and I opened up the scabs on my scratch. A scratch which was inflicted while climbing a tree."

"Sure, sis," Ben said. "I haven't seen you climb a tree since you were eleven. That didn't come from a damn tree and stop covering for him. His type doesn't deserve it."

"I'm not covering for him, and if you so much as lay another hand on him, Ben, I will...I will send all this crap to the junkyard and tell your sweetie you haven't sold a single piece. Do you hear me?"

Todd had no clue what that meant but he assumed Ben had been passing off his artwork as more successful than hoped. Probably for his family's benefit. Or his. Who knew?

"And Tim, I'll tell Mom about your trip to Dayton last spring. I'm sure she'd find that real interesting. Almost as interesting as the grandkid they don't know about!"

Oh my God. It's the Kardashians – in a Latin sort of way. Ben released Todd and switched his snarl to Tim. "What grandkid?"

"Oh shit," Reva muttered and removed a hand from Tim's head to clamp it over her mouth. Tim shrugged her off his back and gave her a snarl that Todd thought might actually wither a weaker person. Not Reva.

"Yeah, oh shit. Thanks, sis. I appreciate you airing my dirty laundry. Any other bombshells you want to drop on us?"

Ben recognized his evasion and persisted. "What grandkid, Tim?"

"None of your damn business." Tim stomped back to Todd, still nursing a battered shin. With a growl, Tim pulled him from the ground and twisted fingers into the neck of his shirt. When they were almost eye-to-eye he spoke. "Did you lay hands on my sister or not?"

Todd looked through the healthy eye and shook his head. The movement sent a shot of pain across his right cheek and he quickly ended his denial.

"Did you cause that scratch?"

Todd looked at the smear of blood on Reva's arm. If he hadn't let her carry the rocks, the wound would have been fine. If his eyes had not been focused on her ass and legs as she flexed to lift the rocks, he'd be a little less bruised. *Way to go, perve.* He started to nod.

She stepped in front of him, noticing his acquiescence before they did. "Of course not, you idiots. He was helping me carry this stuff to the backyard, like I said." Reva waved at the fountain parts. "I scratched my arm in the process. Well, technically I scratched it a while back because I got it stuck in a tree trying to get a baseball. But carrying the rocks opened up the scratches again."

Ben stooped down to evaluate the equipment. "So, you're putting in a fountain, Rev?"

"Yes. Actually, Todd *gave* me the fountain earlier. It's a demo from one of his suppliers and we were going to install it this weekend. Now, it looks like he's going to need a couple days of recovery before we get started, thanks to you two."

Tim and Ben exchanged glances and backed away from Todd. Tim ran a hand down his shirt to smooth it and added, "Sorry about that man. No hard feelings?"

"Reva?" Todd tried to focus her way. "You have any ice in there?" He motioned to her door as he pressed a hand to his eye. He understood Tim and Ben. He knew where they came from and likely might have done the same thing. Still, as much as he liked her and enjoyed her company, this seemed to punctuate his reservations about involvement with a woman that had been through so much. What the hell had convinced him to keep trying?

"Sure. Come on." She took his arm between her hands and led him inside. Ben and Tim followed. "So, now that you've done all the damage you can, mind telling me why you're here?" She spoke over her shoulder at her brothers.

"Uh, we just wanted to stop in and check on you," Ben said.

Reva eyed them suspiciously as she removed a baggie from the cabinet and filled it. She walked to her living room for a minute then returned and placed the ice against Todd's cheek. He sighed at the coolness of the contact which drew the heat and pain away. Home sounded good at the moment. He wanted to lie down for a while, down a beer, and consider how he'd get out of building the fountain.

"Is that one of your sculptures in the back of Tim's truck?" Reva asked Ben.

Tim coughed. Ben shuffled a shoe across in front of the other before he answered. "Um, yeah. I thought I'd swap it for the broken one."

"The broken one's fixed," Todd said.

It was difficult to disguise his annoyance. Todd took the ice bag from Reva's hand and lifted away from her counter. "I had better get home. You guys enjoy your night." He waved and headed toward the door. Todd chastised himself for considering this night would end with his mouth against Reva's. In truth, since the first time he'd seen her getting out of her car, that thought had been on his mind. Now, he realized touching Reva at all might be dangerous, stupid, and complicated. If this had happened just due to a scratch on her arm, imagine what might happen if he'd kissed her and she hadn't wanted him to. Part of him wanted to protect her as they were doing, but in all honesty, another part wanted more than just the role of body guard. Common sense told him all of that was idiotic to consider at all.

Reva reached out and snagged his arm as he passed. "Wait." She looked into his eyes and he imagined she recognized his thoughts. Reva tiptoed to him, brushed the icepack from his cheek, and planted her lips firmly against his. Todd darted a look at her brothers. She pressed into him, molding those delicious curves to him, and he felt the warmth of her skin. His eyes closed involuntarily. She threaded her fingers into his hair and a growing heat passed over him even with the icepack firmly in his hand. Though he wanted to, he didn't dare move his fingers to clutch her skin. Todd feared it would startle her and she'd back off. He leaned into her. She trailed a couple more kisses across his cheek then whispered in his ear, "I'll make this up to you. I promise."

You just did.

Reva pulled back and smiled up at him before letting go. Todd stumbled to the door, tongue-tied. He had not only been punched in the face but her kiss had sucker-punched him as well. He reveled in the feeling of her warm lips on his, her fingers in his hair, and the brief touch of her breasts against his chest. The whole scenario spelled big trouble. Complicated. Idiotic. Trouble.

CHAPTER EIGHT

S pill, kiddo," Tim said after Todd was gone. "First you tell us he's moving in, then he's in your backyard with his hands on you and blood trailed down your arm. Next you're giving him vertical CPR. What's going on?"

"Nothing. Yet. He lives behind me and we play softball together. That's all." Reva wondered if Todd still planned to install the fountain. She wouldn't blame him if he had changed his mind. "Although, now he might press charges against us for assault, thanks to both of you."

"We didn't assault him," Ben denied. Reva simply raised her brows and glanced at him. "Okay, maybe we did but he was—"

"Making a move, asshole," Tim said, recognizing what had transpired. "Reva scratched herself and he had planned to play the big hero but we went all ape-shit and ruined it. Now the poor guy thinks we're all a bunch of crazies. Sorry Rev."

She shrugged. "Well, your heart was in the right place even though your fists weren't."

The remainder of the week Reva struggled to shake the kiss out of her head. Sure, she had instigated it but that was a rash decision made to alleviate the situation. Her brothers thought him an aggressor. They had lumped him in the same category as Nick without thought. She imagined much of that came from their helpless feeling at not being around when things with Nick got nasty. There was little they could have done anyway and Todd was nothing like her ex. She had considered her action a way of redeeming him. Unfortunately, it had served more to confuse her than anything. The kiss hadn't prompted an electrical shock like in a novel, but more a heated need to keep the contact, as if they had been sealed in place. Like a drum roll that needed a cymbal crash after. Reva's own reaction surprised her.

It had been a strange few days, so when Adam wandered into Reva's office at the end of the day on Thursday, she anticipated nothing less than drama. She was right.

"First of all, I don't have a problem working for a woman, if that's what you think," Adam said as he dropped into the chair opposite Reva's desk. Funny, the guy was so positive with the other staff yet the scowl that had ingrained itself in his features was the only expression she had seen in several months. His words, or that thought, had never entered her mind until that moment.

"Well, you certainly have my attention. Hello to you, too." Reva offered a smile that Adam ignored. She glanced at the clock, four minutes to five. "Don't shoot me if I ask you to cut this short. My neighbor signed me up for a softball team and we have practice in forty-five minutes."

Another scowl, followed by a shrug. "Understood." Adam had blondish-brown hair, which sported a cut so short portions of his scalp showed through. If she hadn't known otherwise, she might have thought him an armed services veteran. Six years her junior, the look added age to his appearance, which proved deceptive to the company's staff. Many thought him older than she, when in truth he had only been out of college four and a half years. "Still, do you have a minute to talk?" he asked, not leaving her much choice.

She nodded. "I have about twenty. After that, I have to go."

"Good. Listen, after our discussion the other day, I thought maybe I should just lay everything on the table. Let you know what's going on with me." He lifted a slightly shaky hand to his head and scrubbed it across the back of his neck before continuing. "I've had a lot of trouble with how you speak to me on my projects. Maybe you don't mean it bad, but I'm not taking it well."

"How I speak to you on your projects?" she repeated.

In the past, this type of talk would have caused Reva to erupt. Exactly, who's the boss here? The old Reva would have gotten right in his face and let him have it with both barrels. That woman would have reminded him that though he had been disrespectful and almost combative in some of their meetings, she had waited until they met one-on-one to discuss his behavior and the lack of progress on his projects. But that was the pre-Nick Reva. That woman had been completely confident in herself, and willing to stand up when challenged. And willing to challenge right back if necessary. Post-Nick Reva no longer had that confidence. It had been pummeled out of her. A quick glance to her fingers, which she'd entwined on the desk, showed the slight tremble she knew well. It came before the stillness.

Adam continued. "Yeah, I can't help but feel like I've gotten off on a wrong foot with you. A lot of the things I say, you take—well, wrong. Not like I mean them." Adam went on to list a string of situations where he felt their discussions had either belittled or diminished him. He then explained how he felt in each of those situations. Many of the incidents she remembered completely different or had no recollection of at all. In her recollection, his comments had been tinged with disrespect and challenge. Regardless, she thought his words seemed to display an extreme sensitivity that signified deeper issues. *Holy Moses, do I look like a shrink?* Reva's brothers would have laughed this man off the planet for his sensitivity just as they had done her on more than one occasion when she showed her feminine side a bit too much. They had no concept of empathy. She realized her family had used humor and teasing like some used therapists. In some situations, that worked. But she learned that it could backfire also.

"You with me?" Adam asked. His brows lifted as if he noted her thoughts.

"Sure. I was just trying to remember the conversations you're referencing, as they obviously didn't make the same impression on me they did with you. I have to admit that with a staff of eighteen, I sometimes lose track of every word that's been said, and I probably say things in haste and assume we're on the same page. Still, if you have concerns, you should voice them, so let's hear it." She followed the statement with a smile. It prided Reva that the main thing she had learned from the fiasco with Nick was how to maintain her composure, and diffuse a potential blow-up.

"That's what I'm doing right now," Adam answered. "So, are we good now? Do you have questions about what I said?"

Only one, do you realize you're lying about not having a problem working for a woman? She held her tongue, took four slow breaths and kept her eyes down. This had been a residual trait of her past relationship. She had learned to keep her head down and not challenge Nick by meeting his eyes. She knew Nick's behavior well and this seemed much like it—an effort to control a person and get a desired result. Challenging it verbally, or even in a subtle way, had sometimes led to a raised hand against her cheekbone...or locking her into the closet so that she couldn't storm out. That had been in the past though. Adam wasn't Nick, she reminded herself.

Reva pasted a smile on her dry lips. "No questions, just a few suggestions. First of all, I appreciate you taking the time to come into my office and express your concerns. I have no way of knowing there's an issue if it's not brought to my attention." She reminded herself to use inclusive words, rather than exclusive to share the responsibility and keep it *work-focused.* "Going forward, to make sure that we meet the project's goals, the company's deadline, and not have any further miscommunication, I think we should meet more regularly. I've said this before but we haven't implemented anything. We will meet Tuesdays from now until it becomes unnecessary." She glanced at her calendar on the computer and blocked off times. "Four to five p.m. seems to be a good time for you, so let's do it then. Bring the project plan, plus any other things that need to be discussed. We'll concentrate on progress and issues that may or may not have prevented such progress. Sound good?"

"Yeah sure." He seemed more relaxed.

In truth, Reva had let him talk way too long. The time on her watch glared at her as if to remind her of her tardiness.

"Thanks a lot. I'm glad we had this talk," he said.

"Sure, no problem. Adam, in the future, don't wait so long. If it's bothering you, it's best to get it out in the open rather than let it boil."

"I will."

As soon as he left, she bolted for home and then softball practice. The thought that she had missed a key detail during the interaction nagged her the rest of the evening.

Adam sauntered back to his office, pleased with himself. He had taken the bull (or in this case bitch) by the horns and won. She had sat there quietly as he told her exactly what he thought of her actions and words. She'd said very little and when he finished, she seemed reasonably pleasant about it. She even smiled and thanked him for coming in. It was unlike their past discussions where she had been abrupt and unyielding. Disgracious. That was the word to describe her attitude. She lacked in female grace and manners. No problem, he'd teach her a few.

Sure, his project was delayed but it had taken time to figure out all the details associated with the software. It was a pretty intricate program. He was smarter than most though, and confident he could get things back on track very quickly. She just needed to stop being so impatient. It was damned irritating the way she nagged. It wasn't her responsibility to babysit him. He was more than capable of handling it.

His ex-wife had been like that. Constantly nagging. *When are you coming home? Why do you always have to work late? When are you going to get the tests done?* She wanted kids and had taken the last of her birth control pills more than a year earlier but it didn't seem to "take". Her mood disintegrated over time and he became less and less interested in children— and sex too. Sex for procreation wasn't near as enjoyable as the fun kind. He missed when her focus had been on pleasing him. As far as working late, he didn't. He had just tired of her questions so he started hanging out at the club near the house rather than hurry home. He'd even asked a couple of his teammates at work out for drinks sometimes just to avoid the stark reality of disappointing her. When his wife had finally given up and packed her bags, it had been a relief.

Reva Zamora seemed a genetic mutation of his ex-wife. Bossy, selfish, and totally self-absorbed. All she seemed interested in was how the project reflected on *her*. Yeah, she always said the right words—"we" and "us"—and she talked about how their actions reflected on the team and department. Still, he knew that all she really cared about was whether it made her look bad. Reva was all about...Reva. Their conversation merely dampened the flames of his animosity. It gave him hope though. Perhaps if he kept talking to her on a regular basis, she'd get off his ass and let him do the project the way he wanted to. He was sick of her interfering. He didn't need an entire team of people sticking their noses into this. He could handle it himself. Hell, he enjoyed handling it. Plus, it gave him a chance to communicate with their entire company.

People sought him out. Lately, they'd sought him out even more than boss lady and that gave some smug satisfaction. Back in his office, he stuffed his laptop into the bag behind his chair. Adam slipped his fingers into his pocket and jingled his keys to make sure he hadn't left them in his desk and headed downstairs. He whistled as he took the stairs to the back exit. Taking the stairs had been one of the few attempts to improve his health that stuck. Much of that had been attributed to the slowness of the building's elevators.

Was Reva's newfound patience and kindness a ruse? Perhaps, he speculated, but regardless it gave him a little more distance. With that, he could continue to stay on top of the requests from the rest of the company and not worry. Yeah, she had criticized his announcement to staff that they were starting earlier than she wanted on the project. That was just her way of maintaining control. Why do women always want to have control over you?

Adam pressed the button to unlock the door to his new truck. New was subjective. He'd bought it from the dealership down the road but it had 20,000 miles on it when he took possession. Still, he liked the color, a nice light brown with dark tinted windows that kept the heat out in the summer. He'd had it for six months. A rushed purchase when the lawyers made him turn over the car to his ex as part of the settlement.

Why does everything have to be such a fight?

The battle over the car had taken three months and ended in a compromise: the car for his golf clubs and boat. He wasn't about to let the baby-hungry bitch take everything. The house was hers to begin with. Adam suspected she would have preferred to keep everything simply to take it away from him, but common sense got the best of her. She knew she required transportation to and from work and her job was her life. Or at least it was her biggest priority now that she'd given up on children with him.

Adam turned the key in the truck's ignition and it coughed and sputtered. He growled. Okay. It was a nice looking truck but he still had to take it back and get the engine checked out. It had backfired since the day they delivered it to him. Damned irritating, but he wasn't about to take off work with Reva breathing down his neck.

Reva Zamora is a lunatic. He shouldn't have said that to Gavin a while back. Still, she wasn't exactly the sharpest stick in the pile. Admittedly, she was coming around though. He expected if he continued to talk to her she'd be on his side. She improved almost every time and seemed to understand him better now. Perhaps Gavin's suggestion to talk to her had manifested positive rewards. Time would tell. He mulled over the situation as his cell phone chirped at him.

"This is Adam," he answered in his usual tone. He'd shared his phone number with a lot of staff lately and took great pride in the fact that they called him directly rather than the support number. In fact, he surmised that he'd successfully convinced much of the staff to call him, rather than Reva. He listened smugly as the person on the other phone just changed his plans to go home on time. "Sure, I can help you. I'll be there shortly. Have you called support yet?"

It pleased him that he would likely have to bypass her password again to do what was asked. *Maybe she wasn't a lunatic, but she sure as hell was an idiot when it came to security.* Her password had taken him less than twenty minutes to hack with his software and he doubted she'd changed it in the past thirty days.

CHAPTER NINE

——— ———

On the way to practice, Reva shook the discussion with Adam out of her head and reminded herself that tonight she'd see Todd for the first time since her brothers accosted him. What a disaster. It had not been a pretty sight and she feared he wouldn't speak with her. She had attempted to call him twice without answer. At first, she hoped the kiss had been as interesting for him as for her. When he hadn't answered the phone, she assumed that wasn't the case. Still, as much as she wanted to deny it, she needed a repeat. Of the kiss, not her brothers' antics. Was she really getting that desperate?

Reva ran to the ball field. A quick glance at her watch reinforced that she was late and they had likely already warmed up. Still, she managed to maintain her usual routine caution. Cars cruised by and she avoided them. A few neighbors were out walking their pets after the animals had spent a day penned up. The ballpark lights were on but dusk hadn't fully swallowed the sun yet. The shadows were deep over the field of players.

Reva scanned the group, searching each figure. He wasn't there. Of course not, she reprimanded herself. Why would he show up after what happened? He probably had a hellacious bruised face and ego. Not to mention that she now qualified as a crazy woman with equally crazy family.

"You're late." Todd's voice? Jeff, their team captain posted a line up for their scrimmage on the fence. When he moved away, there on the bench sat Todd. He had bent over tying his cleats before gathering his glove from beside him.

"Yeah. Someone stopped by my office for a chat just as I started to leave. I tried to rush him to finish but no such luck." She squinted at Todd's face. Yellow and gray marks showed faintly on the swollen cheekbone below his eye. Reva felt a stab of regret and squelched an urge to touch it. "How are you doing?"

"Sheesh, who won?" Jeff asked as he noticed Reva's bandaged arm and Todd's bruised face. He laughed and anticipated they would join him in the humor. They didn't. "Uh, sorry." He shuffled to the field and gathered everyone up to start batting practice.

"I'm good. You?" Todd answered. He pounded his fist into the supple baseball leather on his hand. Well, he showed up. That had to be a good sign. Right? The bruise proved less severe than expected. She wondered if it felt tender to the touch. The urge surfaced again to stroke a finger across the lump and she sighed.

"Fine. Guess I'd better get out there." Reva grabbed a bat and rushed out to take first hits. A quick glance over her shoulder as she exited the dugout caught Todd's eyes firmly planted on her pockets as he sauntered to his position in the field. She moved to home plate suppressing a grin. Okay, the conversation was awkward but maybe there was still hope. She had no idea what for, but she'd figure that out later. After all, she had no interest in men at the moment. Although it had become a bit harder to convince herself after kissing him.

Wolf whistles from the stands caught her attention. Great. Some sleaze ball intended to make a scene. Really? "Knock the hell out of it, Rev!" Tim's voice. It had to be. She turned to look just as the pitch flew past her.

"Strike," Jeff called. "Good thing this is just practice. That pitch was served up perfectly and you let it go. Pay attention."

What the hell is Tim doing here? Had he become so protective that he intended to follow her around as if she were twelve? Reva frowned and burrowed her head in concentration as the next pitch approached. She nailed it. It was a nice line drive right down the third base line and she made it to second.

"Woo! Way to go, sis!" And that was Ben. *Unbelie*
They both had showed up? Obviously, they hadn't believ
story about Todd and intended to make their prote
presence known.

Todd had been assigned to take shortstop and he grinne
way. "Looks like you have a cheering squad."

"Don't you mean bodyguards?" She snorted.

"Basically the same thing, isn't it?"

Jeff was second up and hit a fly ball to the outfield, se
Reva around the remaining bases before George in the ou
made a diving catch, then rolled and sailed the ball back
pitcher. The guy had a great arm but seriously, who r
their kid George nowadays? Reva rationalized it had tc
family name. They continued until everyone had a chai
bat twice. Another team showed up to scrimmage and
took the field. The game lasted about an hour with Tir
Ben whistling and cheering like it was the minor leagues.
laughed and carried on like kids. Reva stepped closer
fence at one point and shushed them.

"Quit acting like idiots. It's just a scrimmage.'
narrowed her eyes and took in the beer cans unde
bleachers. "Oh. No wonder. You two are seriously bu
Time to go home—both of you." She wiggled a finger
one to the other.

"Nah. We're just getting warmed up. Besides we said
stay till it was over," Tim said.

"Well, I don't need you to stay. Scratch that. I don't
you to stay." She pointed to the parking lot. "Go."

"No can do, little sista," Ben teased. "You're stuck wi
Now get back out there. Your team needs you, slugger –
swooshed a dismissive hand, "and tell that coach of your
if he pats you on the ass one more time, I might have to
out there and beat his." They both burst out laughing.

Reva growled. "Shut up, or at least keep your voices d
She punched a finger at both of them to punctuate her v
and returned to the team.

In the fourth inning, Reva hit a grounder that bounced
the pitcher's mound and landed conveniently in the short
glove. He subsequently threw her out at first and receive

scolding from her brothers. The scrimmage ended after five innings with the teams tied.

The other team's catcher, an athletic but attractive blonde, approached as she packed her bag. "Your family's cute," she said. "They might need a ride home, though."

Wonder where she got that idea. Reva acknowledged her brothers' lack of musical talent as they screamed "Take me out to the ball game" while swaying side to side on the aluminum bleacher. Yep, they needed a ride...and a cup of coffee—correction, a gallon of coffee—each.

CHAPTER TEN

Reva felt Todd standing behind her before he said a word. His scent was deliciously familiar even with a little sweat added to the mix. "Can you believe this?" she asked. "I can't take a step without a family member under foot. I don't know why they think I need to be followed around."

"They care about you. That's not so bad, is it?"

"No, but I'd rather they do it at home. I didn't ask them to come up here and make a scene screaming at the top of their lungs."

"No, you sure didn't."

"And I don't want them sticking their noses in my business. Who invited them to butt in anyway?"

"I did." He moved next to her.

"Huh?"

"I invited them."

"Really?"

"Yep. They called to apologize for the other night." He turned to Reva. "I told them if they were that concerned, they should come watch our practice and see just how things really are. Of course, I hadn't planned on this." He waved at the two burly guys in shorts.

"So, I have *you* to blame for the two drunks in the stands?" Reva asked.

He laughed. "No, they brought the beer. I just told them

where we'd be. I didn't know they intended to make a party of it."

"At least Mom and Dad aren't with them. Dad's the worst when it comes to obnoxious fans. Those guys don't even come close." She hooked a thumb toward the bleachers, noticing that her brothers had left.

Still, she loved the lugs and had missed them when she had been too far away for their visits. Growing up, their constant ribbing and interference had been a staple in her life. In Maria's too. She'd found it frustrating when she was younger but now, as much as she complained—she appreciated the sentiment behind their actions. She wondered if their meddling would have helped with Nick, had she stayed.

Duh. She'd have never met the asshole if she'd stayed.

A breeze lifted Todd's hair from his brow and tossed it from his face. Reva peeled her eyes away and dropped her glove into the sports bag. She flipped the bag over a shoulder. Time for a subject change. "Well, our first game is tomorrow. That should be fun. We'll see just how good we really are."

"Or aren't," Todd answered.

She smiled. "True, but a little pessimistic. See you then." Reva turned to leave. The few cars around the ball field had begun to depart. Ben and Tim rolled a cooler to the trashcan, tossed their empty cans, then loaded it into Ben's truck. They sat on the bed of the vehicle, eyes on their sister's approach.

"You played pretty good for a girl," Ben joked. He nodded to Todd. "He wasn't so bad either."

Reva grinned. "I bet I could still whip both of you if it came to that, but I know you're both too chicken to try to take me." She put a hand on her hip and felt sweat trickle down the side of her face.

Tim reached into the cooler and pulled two beer cans from it. Reva marveled that there were any left to retrieve. He popped the tab on one and passed it to her. "We're not chicken Reva, but we're not stupid either. You played softball from the time you were nine. When you weren't on the ball field, you were running track or cross country. Neither Ben nor I were into baseball, so any attempt to keep up with you would have been a losing battle. Not to mention the fact that you're a bit younger than both of us. Besides, Todd here seemed to do just fine." Tim passed the other can to Todd as he approached.

"I can hold my own. You guys want to walk back with us?" Todd suggested.

Reva recognized that he'd inferred an *us* that made her uncomfortable. There wasn't any us with Todd. There was him and then her. Separate. Not together. He just...just...oh, why try to explain it? "Are you inviting them to your house or mine?" She asked.

"Doesn't matter. It depends on how much everyone wants to walk. I'm one block farther away."

"Judging on the way these two were singing, I'd guess the extra exercise might do them some good. You know with the fresh air and all."

Tim frowned. "What are you trying to say now?" He ran a hand down his flat-as-a-pancake stomach and patted.

"Just that you probably need to dry out a little before you think about driving that truck. Don't worry, I wasn't calling you fat or inferring you had a beer-gut. Yet."

Tim and Ben slid off the truck bed, and followed Reva and Todd. She noticed Tim's prolonged glance at the pretty blonde from the other team.

Two brothers would have been heaven, Todd thought as he remembered sharing a bathroom with his older sister. He wondered what it had been like for them as children. For him, it had been pure torture. Undergarments consistently hung over the towel bar, make-up and hair dryer scattered over the bathroom counter. Where he had been meticulous and organized, she had been everything but. It more than annoyed him to snag a pile of her nasties from the bathroom floor and toss them into her room. He hadn't cared what she did in her own space, but he refused to let Terry's laziness creep into his. Nor into the spaces they had shared through their teenage years. She had found it a game.

He looked out over the park and reminisced that he wished for that frustration now. His sister had married and moved an ocean away to be with her husband and his new job. It worked out well for her since they were both journalists. As much as she annoyed him then, their biweekly conversations were a blessing. Reva complained but Todd sensed her appreciation for the two somewhat inebriated human guard dogs behind her. He had no doubt that even in that state, they boded trouble for any man that meant harm for the beautiful woman at his side. He shot a glance sideways. Yes, beautiful. Even with sweat trickling down her neck and dirt smattered across the pockets of those tight shorts. Reva's brothers had their work cut out for them.

"Did you eat before practice?" he asked.

"I didn't have time. I have some leftovers in the fridge, though."

He noticed she glanced around the street. Always kept an eye on her surroundings. She had perfected the art of being present yet separate. He purposely stepped closer just to see what happened. Nothing. Wait. Ah, she added distance, a little safety.

"I'll fire up the grill and feed all of you tonight. I have everything for burgers if that's okay," he said.

"I...um. Sure. Just long enough for them to get some air in their lungs and food in their stomachs, though. I have some work to do. I had a personnel issue this afternoon that I need to document while it's still fresh in my mind."

He didn't respond. A personnel issue. Her work seemed plagued with those. That was something he rarely had to deal with in his own business. Since he owned the whole thing, no one gave him grief. In fact, just the opposite. His business had blossomed and the few people he'd added over the past few years were long-time acquaintances and friends. People he trusted to be as dedicated as he, himself with his dream. They came to work with energy and enthusiasm every day and knew, without a doubt, that their contributions *mattered*. He had no need to constantly assure them. They knew. That was the beauty of a small enterprise rather than a larger environment such as hers. Fewer personalities, therefore fewer personality differences—in his opinion, of course. It had also meant that everyone had pulled their weight and more. Just last night, he had been at the office/shop/warehouse to help package a large shipment and get the billing done.

Should he be concerned that she had escaped an abusive relationship in her recent past, and had personnel issues that required documentation? What, exactly, did that infer? He had never documented any of the few incidents he encountered at work. He'd done so intentionally. Much of the time it was for the benefit of his staff but he also felt it best not to constantly rehash old troubles. Documenting such became a permanent smear for the person involved. As a result, he chose only to document the good—and often skipped that too. Instead he made sure he talked them up when they excelled and made them aware when they didn't. Periodic adjustments in their pay substantiated their effort. When he could afford it, of course. It seemed appropriate to do both and it worked. So far. An attorney would likely argue his methods but he didn't care. One can't base decisions on the remote possibility of lawsuits.

Burgers with Reva and her brothers was hilarious. They mercilessly teased everyone and it seemed obvious they had the wrong impression about his relationship with Reva, which wasn't a relationship at all. He had no clue what it was, but definitely not that. Todd admitted that Tim and Ben had the type of easy confidence that was compelling. Had he known them growing up, they likely would have been friends. Had he not been completely immersed in work these past few years, these were the kind of people he would have enjoyed spending time around.

Two hours later, the burgers had been demolished. Tim and Ben had walked back to their truck in much better condition than before. Todd appreciated that they seemed comfortable enough with him to leave Reva, although he did notice a private interchange between them as they departed. Reva grabbed tea glasses, paper plates, strewn trash, and carried them to his back door.

Todd realized that the whole of his early years, he had been obsessed with achievement. His obsession had taken root and blossomed. The success of his business wasn't a fluke. It had come with pain, sweat, and a lot of late night hard work. It had also come with a price and while he hated to admit it, there was a tinge of loneliness and alienation that lurked in the fringes of his life. He rarely acknowledged it as he normally just covered himself up in work when he did. Tonight, though, as he watched Reva with her brothers, it hit him hard. This was what he had missed. What Todd had hoped for in his family life since he left home to conquer college and then the world. What had never really quite happened with Annie. The only bright spot in all that had been Eric. Apparently, he'd never *understood* her.

"I've put the dirties in the dishwasher and bagged the trash. I left the bag by the door as I wasn't sure where to put it." Reva smiled. "Thanks for feeding us. I'd better get back and write up that report."

"Need help with it? I'm great with words."

"You wouldn't enjoy this. I had a staff member voice his displeasure with the way I speak with him. Since this isn't the first time he's had a problem, I thought I'd better write it down just in case something comes of it."

"What's his problem?" He didn't mean it to sound critical but recognized it did.

"Apparently my tone of voice. Or at least how I say what I say, rather than the actual words. If that makes sense." The lines between her eyebrows dented as he watched her frown.

"He sounds hyper-sensitive."

"Maybe. I don't know. Isn't everyone hyper-sensitive about something at some point? Anyway, I need to write it down while it's still fresh. I'll admit I can be abrupt at times. Mainly because I believe in stating the facts, outlining what needs to be done, and then doing it. It frustrates me when people don't do what you ask of them. It especially frustrates me when they pretend to know something they don't and then screw things up because their ego won't let them ask for help. But that's only part of the issue, as far as I'm concerned. If someone asks a question, I assume they want my opinion and an answer. I give it and most times, I don't sugar coat it. That's where this particular person has an issue. Personally, I think he's not comfortable with a woman expressing opinions and giving direction quite so bluntly. I can't say that though. That would be discriminatory."

"Discriminatory in pointing out that he's discriminating against you as a female in business, and let's not forget you're his boss? Or that it's very likely he can take the exact same words from a man but not from you?"

"Ah, you get it. That's the dilemma in this. If I point out his prejudices, it sounds as if I am prejudiced against him. As a boss, that's a huge no-no. So, even though I know much of his anger toward me wouldn't exist if I were a man saying the same things...in truth, as a man, I could be even stronger and he'd be fine with it. I also know it would be disastrous to my credibility and career to point out the obvious. Plus, and this is the big one, I didn't get this far by complaining about how I'm treated in my work and I sure as hell am not going to start crying wolf now."

"So, in other words, you're letting him have the upper hand?"

"No, I'm documenting it. Word for word. Should problems continue and his projects don't get back on track, he will be officially reprimanded and I'll have the data to support it."

Todd sighed. "And if he documents it differently, then what happens? People can write whatever they want to on paper, that doesn't necessarily make it fact—or even honest. I'm so glad I don't work in the corporate realm anymore."

Her eyes widened in surprise. "But you do. You're a business owner and an entrepreneur. That's about as corporate as it gets."

"No, that's small business. No fancy offices, no big staff, and only a few corporate policies, none of which take precedence over common sense. If I had an employee like that working for me, well, he wouldn't work for me long."

Reva shot her head up and her eyes flashed. "Why? Because you're a man and you can handle it better?"

"No. Because I'm a man and he wouldn't try that shit with me. It wouldn't work. Don't you see?"

"That's my point! That's exactly what's wrong. I should be able to say exactly the same things that any man in my position would and expect him to do his job. I can't and he doesn't."

"Then fire him."

"Without even giving him a chance to correct things? That would be cruel."

"That's business. He would do the same to you if the tables

were turned."

"But they're not, are they? I have to believe that our legal system and our generation make it possible for both of us to be successful. Not in an *I win, you lose* way either. I want him to resolve the problems on his project. I want him to stop being so concerned with what I say or how I say it, but what needs to get done and how to do it. And I especially want him to stop making mistakes and overpromising to the staff. If he doesn't, I'm prepared to make a change but I'd rather not. Any time you change personnel, there's a huge learning curve to get past. That will delay his projects even further. So, I'm keeping my hands in it deep enough to take over if needed but still give him room to fix it."

"You should tell him that. Exactly like that. If he doesn't get it, then he doesn't want to."

"Then I fail?"

"No, Reva. It's not about failure. It's about success. If he doesn't understand what you tell him, then he's only concerned about his own success and you can't afford that. Or at least that's how I see it."

"He scares me." Her face and body stilled in a "calm before the storm" way as she spoke. "I'm overreacting I know, but something about him reminds me of the past."

"You mean of your ex? Jesus, Reva. That's not even remotely funny."

"It's not meant to be. I know it's a stretch. I shouldn't have said it. See? I'm overreacting." She pulled the tie from her hair, smoothed the lose strands into place, then tied it all up again. The simple act seemed to normalize her words.

"Reva, I don't know a lot about you but I do know you're a smart woman. I'd bet you're very good at your work." He sensed she needed confirmation. He stepped toward her in his small kitchen. Did he think she had overreacted based on prior experience? He had no idea. In truth, he had no understanding of women in business at all. Obviously. Yet, in a way he understood exactly. She wanted this employee to turn things around. She wanted him to succeed. Todd doubted the employee wanted the same for her.

"Okay, I'm giving you warning that I'm going to touch you

now." He'd been increasingly aware of Reva's evasiveness through the night. Whenever he moved closer, she countered by adding distance. Sometimes it was small. Other times, it was significant. She did so in an unobtrusive natural way. Still, he noticed. He had eased closer and if she was comfortable it remained that way for a while. Then, as if a lock clicking shut, she would perform some small action that added space to her comfort zone. During their conversation, he had eased to her side and she hadn't moved. It was a stupid cat and mouse game and he wondered why he bothered to play it. The kiss, of course. She'd gone at him with a hunger he found seductive.

He inched his hands up to cup her face. She looked at his wrists. He waited. And waited. "Reva. Look up."

"What?" She stared at his nose.

"A little more." Her eyes met his. "There. See, not so bad right? Look, not every guy is abusive. Maybe this guy's attracted to you..."

She let out a laugh. He tightened his grip just slightly.

"Don't laugh. It makes sense."

"You're a psychiatrist now?"

He kept his hands in place and wouldn't allow her to back up. "No. I'm trying to understand why he might be difficult as an employee. That's what you did, didn't you? You tried to find a reason, an excuse for his obvious disrespect of your authority."

"Yes."

"I usually don't care. That's why women make better managers as a general rule. They care more."

"I don't see that as a plus. If I didn't care, I would have fired him and moved on."

"But you can't do it. And I'd bet you didn't because you know how hard it is for a person to recover from a firing and move on with their life." He watched her face. Bingo.

"Yes."

He smiled. "Reva, that's why you're a good manager. You make decisions not only on what's best for your company but also what's best for the staff. Even if they don't recognize it as that."

She rolled her eyes and spoke. "How much do I owe you for

that wonderful evaluation and advice, Yoda?"

"Put it on my tab, and Reva?" He waited for her to slide her eyes back to his.

"Hmmm?"

"I'm going to kiss you now."

CHAPTER ELEVEN

——— ———

Reva studied Todd with trepidation. How had she talked so easily with him about such an emotionally charged situation and he hadn't flared up? He accepted her thoughts as if they were right. As if they made sense. He didn't tell her she was unreasonable, nor that she imagined the situation. More importantly he didn't tell her she was wrong. He didn't make her feel stupid or worthless.

"You're listening to me," she stated bluntly as he came closer. The look of surprise on his face interested her.

"Isn't that what you wanted?"

"Yes, but I didn't expect — You didn't discredit what I said."

"Why would I do that? Those are normal feelings that any decent boss has. Any decent person really." He shrugged. "Mind if we get back to where I was a second ago—you know, the kissing part?"

"Oh, um..." Reva smiled and he lowered his head to her. His mouth touched gentle against hers. Considering that he'd listened and treated her kindly, it was the least she could do. Let him kiss her. Besides, the first kiss had been amazing. She stood still as he leaned into her and slipped a hand to rest on her shoulder. The other slid behind her to grip her hair. Nice. She resisted the urge to back up. Her stomach rumbled.

"Don't run off. I'm not going to hurt you."

She let the tenseness in her neck slip away, her shoulders

loosened. When he moved tighter against her, it felt natural. Okay, maybe there was nothing wrong with giving in. Admittedly, she found him attractive. Very. And if this kiss was any indication of his other talents, she had the impression he'd be quite good at whatever he decided.

"Relax," he said against her lips. "It's just a kiss."

She groaned and lifted a hand to surround the one he'd placed on her cheek. "Is it?"

"You tell me."

He drew back and slid hands down to lightly clasp her fingers. One step back for distance and she felt better. It bothered her that her body wanted to step into him, even knowing that it might be disappointed—as she had been disappointed so many times before with Nick. The intimacy had always been short-lived and often, if withheld, masked a darker feeling. Did she really want that? Was that why this felt hard to resist? She wanted him to be angry or harsh? Surely, she had not become that warped?

She shrugged. "I should go. I still have work to do."

A vehicle backfired one street over. Her street. It startled them both. "I'll walk with you."

"No. I'm not...going to sleep with you."

"Just to the corner." He smiled. "It's dark and I'd feel better if I knew you made it back okay."

That was nice. "All right. To the corner."

Todd released one hand, retained his grip on the other, and grabbed her baseball gear as they left. Equally nice. She didn't tug away. When they reached the end of his street and turned toward the corner, he spoke. "Why'd you kiss me the other night?"

"I don't know. I was mad. They were interfering. You were aggravated—with me or them. I wasn't sure. I was just tired I guess. I'm sorry."

"No. Don't be. That's not what I meant. It's just – it was different then. I suppose that was the real you. Challenging and aggressive. This, tonight, seemed different."

"I'm sorry."

"Jesus, stop apologizing Reva. I'm not angry or disappointed or anything else. But I can tell when someone is holding back. I've done enough of it to know that much."

"I'm sure you have. I'm—"

He tugged her hand. "Don't you dare say you're sorry again. Look, not every guy gets mad when a girl expresses her opinion. I like it that you told me what you did. I understand it. Can I say that I've felt exactly the same? I don't know. I'm not you, so while I think I get what's bothering you, I can't say for sure. But I'm definitely not him either, and it frustrates me that you seem to be expecting that from me."

"Expecting what?"

"That I'd lose my temper, yell, hit, or tell you something that diminishes you. Maybe get angry with you for talking about it. Or, hell, I don't know."

"I'm not very good at all this, Todd. I don't want a guy around all the time. I certainly don't want a relationship."

"Good. Neither do I. Want a guy around all the time that is." He grinned. "A girl maybe, I don't know. Just so you know, we just kissed. It wasn't a big deal."

Reva surveyed her yard and front porch, noting that she hadn't turned on the light before leaving. She hated to fumble for the keys outside in the open. She pulled the zipper on her bag.

"I didn't think it was." She knelt with him next to her and dug for the keys. "It's fine, Todd. I'm fine." Keys in hand, she stood and offered a smile. "Thanks for tonight. It was nice. And thanks for getting my brothers to lighten up. I think they liked you."

"What's not to like?" He grinned.

Agreed. Todd bent and kissed her cheek lightly. He hesitated then dropped to her lips and pressed another light kiss there too. What's not to like? Nothing. It's a different emotion altogether. Fear, maybe? No, I know that one all too well. This was different, more – exciting. More dangerous.

"Good night, Reva. You're quite a girl."

It took several hours and numerous edits to finish her write-up of the discussion with Adam. At first, she typed word for word and added her thoughts and reactions. Upon the reading of it, she surmised that it had too much personal emotion in it, and she stripped out some of the extra details. It needed to be factual, not her supposition of his thoughts, nor a rehash of her emotions in response to his words. She debated writing an account of the conversation she'd overheard between Gavin and Adam earlier. Naw. She decided to stick to first party conversations only. Once it was done, she saved the file on her laptop, double-checked the locks on the doors, and went to sleep.

You're quite a girl.

Was that good?

Three weeks passed, Reva fell into a routine at work, and after. The Tuesday meetings with Adam had little relevance. He often skipped. At fairly regular intervals, he had wandered into her office between 4:30 and 5:00 to give a status update. He seemed positive, and while his project hadn't progressed as much as hoped, it did move. Since his effort seemed significantly improved, she decided not to continue documenting each discussion. The process of doing so had been cumbersome and unnecessary. Why would anyone choose to be a Human Resources person? Expecting the worse and documenting trivial things in order to protect the organization against litigation seemed the ultimate negativity in relationship management.

The fact that Adam had felt comfortable talking to her was a big step. A good one. She hoped it changed his perspective and that the animosity she heard in the discussion with Gavin had passed. Perhaps it meant that he had accepted the idea that her desire to help him succeed was behind her actions, but that it was contingent on the success of the project as well. Most importantly, she hoped it meant he would make more progress going forward. In the past, he'd been a very energetic employee. Somewhere in the recent few months, he'd lost that. Gavin had mentioned a divorce. Perhaps that was the issue.

That Saturday morning, Maria called, another routine that had developed over the past months since her arrival.

"Hey, Sis. You doing anything—"

"Illegal? No, but if you don't come up with a new line, I might consider it." Reva smiled at the handset.

"Okay. So, I'm a creature of habit. Sue me. You still seeing Todd?"

"I'm not *seeing* anyone. Wow, you don't waste any time do you? Is that all you care about, my love life? Don't bother to ask me something about my job or maybe just about me." Maria had no idea about her work. Whenever Reva started talking technical projects and project management, Maria's eyes glazed over.

"Face it, Reva. Your job isn't that exciting. And you—well, other than softball, it doesn't sound like you have much else to talk about. Speaking of...how is the team working out? Mom said she and Dad have been at the games with Tim and Ben. She said you're the star of the show as far as the girls." Did she sound envious?

"Hardly the star. I don't think some of the other girls have played before. They just signed up because their husbands or boyfriends wanted them to and I'm glad they're playing. It's fun. It's also easy to look decent when it's not competitive."

"Come on. You know you're a born athlete. That's probably what pissed Nick off so much. You were better than him at almost everything."

"Not everything."

She had a point though. In the beginning, Nick seemed to admire her talents. When they did anything at all sporty, he feigned appreciation. He had jogged with her in the beginning and they tried bicycle races as well. He often complimented her on her muscle tone and strength. Then it became another thing to criticize. *You're starting to look like a guy*, he had said when she hoisted a bag of groceries from the car once. *Tone it back a little, muscles like that aren't sexy.*

Sexy? Like she cared. That goal had not been on her mind when she jogged daily, nor when she did the strength training exercises every other day. All that it had been was a way to get outside of herself and think. Dwell on problems and find solutions as well as preserve her health.

"Hello? You still there?" She jolted back to the present. "I didn't mean to dredge that up. Sorry."

"It wasn't like that," Reva answered, but she lied. Maria's perception was dead on. Nick had not liked being bested. He tended to equate winning at sports to his success as a man, or even a person. In addition to a thousand other things. There was very little that met his approval.

"It doesn't matter. That's history. Back to the present – and Mr. Gorgeous and Fatherly. What's up with him?"

Reva heard a car backfire and stood to glance out the window. The same noise interrupted her thoughts on a regular basis lately. She wondered which neighbor needed to get some engine work done. A tan Chevy pickup with tinted windows rolled by. Hmmm. Hadn't seen that one before. Must be new.

"Nothing's up. He's a neighbor. We play softball on the neighborhood team together."

"And you plant hot kisses on him in front of Ben and Tim. Who are you trying to kid, girl? Did you think they wouldn't tell me? I'm happy for you."

"Don't get all excited and start making plans. It was a one-time thing. Well, technically a two-time thing."

"Two times. Kissing? Or the horizontal cha-cha? Ohhhhh, you better tell," Maria scolded.

"I guess Mom's not listening in now." Horizontal Cha-cha? What a ridiculous phrase. No way would Maria ask if they had an eavesdropper. Reva rolled her eyes and stared at the pickup that idled in front of the house two doors down. Maybe it was a boyfriend of the teen that lived there. She turned back to the kitchen and pulled the milk from the fridge.

"Look, Mar, I can't tell you anything because I *don't know* anything. We kissed a couple times. He walked me back from practice a few nights just to be nice. That's about it. I think we scared him."

"We? You mean at the barbecue? Understandable. You both scared all of us, too."

"No. I mean that plus Tim and Ben jumping him. They didn't tell you *that*, did they? Oh yeah, and one of you telling him all my baggage. Thanks for that by the way. Any chance he might have found me normal went out the window that very moment. Then there was getting stuck in the tree and Ben and Tim's continuous drinking at the games. Have they ever considered cutting back a little?" Reva took a breath and ticked off a few other things in her head.

"Hey, they don't *continuous* anything. They just have fun. Screw him if he doesn't like it. Surely he's not that much of a stick in the mud? What's this about a tree?"

"Well, let's just say I've made an impression. What kind, who the hell knows, but something." Reva's doorbell rang. "Gotta go. Someone's at the door." She really hadn't wanted to discuss Todd. There had been little to talk about the past few weeks. He spoke when they practiced. He walked her back, but then he left. Left her wondering.

She yanked the door open and stared out. When no face instantly appeared, she readjusted her vision downward to— "Hey, Eric! What have you been up to?"

"Hi, Ms. Zamora."

"Did Bugsy make an escape again? Do you need to retrieve him? Come on." She motioned for Eric to follow her through to the backyard. She glanced down the street. Todd let him walk over alone?

"No, Bugsy's fine. Dad fixed his cage so he couldn't get out. He's not very happy about it, but at least I don't have to worry about him getting eaten by Mr. Reardan's dog." Eric pointed at the house to her immediate right.

"Good point. So, what's up then?" Reva turned and planted her hands on her hips.

"Nothing. Did Dad call? He told me to come over here. He said he'd call you. He's at work. Mom dropped me off and left."

"She left without checking to see if he was there?" *What kind of mother deposits her kid on the doorstep and just vanishes?*

"No, she called but when he answered, they fought and she got in the car so I wouldn't hear. I went up on the step and took the key out of his hiding place and let myself in."

Wow, this kid is too mature for his own good.

"That's a smart thing to do."

"Yeah. He kind of told me that if I ever needed him to just come over and—he showed me what to do. Anyway, I got a juice out of the fridge and when I went back outside, she was gone."

"Your mom, right?"

"Yeah. So I called Dad. He has the number on the front of the fridge and I have a cell phone that he bought me just in case. It's got his number on it." Reva looked at the battered screen that he pulled from his pocket.

"You're pretty young for a cell phone."

"I take good care of it. I'm smart."

"That's for sure. And you knew what to do. When's Todd—" Reva's cell danced on the kitchen counter where she had dropped it when she answered the door.

Todd. "Reva, I'm sorry to ask but I need your help."

"He's already here."

"Oh good. I can't believe she just dumped him. What a shitty mother. Can you keep him? I'll be back in a couple of hours. We have a big shipment we're trying to get out today. She didn't call and he hasn't been over in a while." He sounded rushed.

"It's fine. Do what you have to do."

"Thanks. You're awesome. It won't be long, a couple hours max." The phone went dead.

Eric wandered around, evaluating the room. "Your house is so much nicer than Dad's."

"Why do you think that?" His house was twice as big. Funny what kids say.

"You have pictures and stuff." Eric pointed to the colorful rug under the kitchen table and her bright pictures over the sofa. The boxes on the shelves by the window caught his attention and without asking he opened them. The pictures inside disappointed and he slipped the lid back. "You got any toys?"

"Not really. I have some paint and stuff though. Have you eaten this morning, Eric? I'm hungry."

"No, Mom woke me up and brought me straight here. She was in a hurry." He stuck his hands in his pockets like Todd did when he seemed unsure where to put them.

"How about some toast then?" He wrinkled his nose. "French toast with syrup. It's like pancakes."

That caught his attention.

Two hours later Todd strolled into the backyard. Reva's speakers blared Disney music and she didn't hear his approach. Two towels spread on the grass gave away their endeavor as they splattered paint on them. Eric had graced his with handprints and footprints of bright blue. Reva's was more refined. Big refined splotches of red, yellow, and orange. She hadn't liked the idea of washing the color off her feet, or trying to explain it so she had simply tossed the paint at the towel with an artful flick of the wrist.

"Hey buddy." Todd's voice startled her and she whirled around. A small shriek escaped before she switched off the music. She wondered how long he had watched. Had he seen her silly dancing to the music? He grinned. *Yes, he'd seen it.*

"That's not going to appear on YouTube is it?" she asked.

"Wish I'd thought of that. I was too busy enjoying the picture." Eric brushed his blue fingers together and started to hug Todd. Quick reflexes prevented blue stains on Todd's pants but the shirt hadn't been as lucky.

Reva flinched. "Oops. Sorry about that. Come on Eric. Let's get you washed off." She picked him up and carried him in an arm lock to the water hose. A quick twist of the faucet turned on the water and she went inside for soap and a towel.

"Looks like you had fun," Todd remarked on her return.

"Well, I'm not equipped very well for entertaining the younger generation. So, I opted for what I found. Craft paint and towels. It should wash out of your shirt if we soak it right away. It sets with heat though. So, if we don't hurry, you're going to stay blue." She held out a hand for the shirt. "Hand it over."

"You just want to see me na—" Todd stopped and glanced at Eric as he growled at the blue water that trailed off his feet in puddles.

"This is a G-rated yard now, but yeah, you caught me." Reva shook her hair out of her face to avoid stroking it back with orange fingers. "Like I said, hand it over." She snapped her fingers.

Todd drew the T-shirt over his head and tossed fabric into the orange hand. He raised a brow and Reva knew he doubted it would be the same again.

"Your stomach's blue, Dad." Eric pointed. Todd looked down and laughed. The blue paint had seeped through the cloth and branded him with blue splotches across the pecks. He had soft lapis-colored hairs over his heart that filtered to a dark brown toward his jeans. Even the odd color didn't squelch Reva's uncomfortable desire to touch them.

"So are you, bud. Let's go home and take a shower."

Reva liked the two of them together. They had an easy affection that comforted her. An affection that was based on trust and a lot more. Todd had never laid a hand on this child. She was certain. That knowledge made him incredibly desirable.

"Why don't you just climb in my shower? By the time you get home, it would dry and probably crust a nice tattoo. There's soap and everything in there, a loofa too. That might scrub the color off. Sorry about the mess. I didn't really think this through, I guess." She stood.

"It's okay, Reva," Todd said. He reached for her arm.

Eric bounced from foot to foot as he admired his work. "I liked painting. That was awesome Miss Zamora! Can I keep the towel?" He noticed Todd's hand on her arm and smiled.

"Of course! It's yours. Let me iron it so the color sets while you two clean up. Then we'll have some lunch. Okay?" She cast a glance to Todd. He nodded.

Todd tugged Eric's shirt up. It caught briefly on his head then released. A white shirt emblazoned with a kid's team name, now covered in blue. He tossed it to Reva. She caught the cloth mid-air and turned toward the sink.

"Wait." Todd blurted. "Don't wash it out. Would you mind ironing those with the towels?"

"But they're covered in blue paint. They're ruined. I can get it out if we hurry and wash them."

He swallowed and she thought his eyes glistened. "I don't want you to wash it out." She spread out the shirts on the counter and stood back.

"Are you sure?"

"Reva, I may not get much more of this with him. If Annie marries this guy—let's just say every day or weekend is a gift. This," Todd waved his hand toward the shirts, "is a gift. It's something he'll remember and so will I. We're keeping the shirts exactly as they are."

Todd's eyes lowered and he pointed at her breasts. "You may want to wash that though." He grinned. "Eric's a hugger."

Two blue splotches strategically placed. "Oh my God." Reva blushed.

Todd's lips twitched. She watched him struggle to control the laughter.

"Quite a fashion statement. I think there's hand prints on your back too." He turned, scooped Eric up, and carried him to the bathroom. The child wiggled and giggled all the way. From the bathroom Todd shouted, "I'll pay for your shirt if you iron that in for me too. Hell, I'll iron them all myself if you give me a few minutes."

"Daddy, you said a bad word."

"I know. Sorry."

She heard the water running just before the door closed. Reva went to her room and changed into a clean bra and shirt. The tenseness in her neck and back fell away. Todd wasn't mad. He hadn't yelled at Eric for getting it all over him. He didn't get upset with her either. Additionally, he looked hot as hell without a shirt and smeared in blue paint. How wonderful that this moment had meant so much to the man! She hugged herself.

CHAPTER TWELVE

——— ———

Todd stripped Eric, lathered soap into the loofa, and began scrubbing the blue coating from his skin. Yeah, it's semi-water soluble. Good thing it hadn't reached his face or he'd look as if he had a health problem. The paint left his skin a faint purplish hue. Still, Eric had enjoyed it. Not just enjoyed it, he bubbled. As the shower flowed over his face, Eric rambled on and on about the picture. Apparently there had been a method to the handprints.

"Dad, did you see the horses? I used my hands to make them." The shower water had cleared somewhat.

"You did a great job."

"And the grass under them? Did you see how I made it go up around their feet?"

"Hooves. Horses don't have feet, they have hooves, Eric." *Might as well use the opportunity to teach something.* "They don't have hands either, and no fingers or toes but they do have teeth. Maybe we'll go ride some when there's time."

"Maybe. Uh, I don't know how."

"Then, you'll learn. It's not that hard. You just have to be careful. We'll try it sometime."

"Can Ms. Zamora go with us? Does she know how?"

Todd lathered Eric's hair, rinsed it, and wrapped him in a towel. "I'm not sure if she does or not. Put your clothes on and go ask. Let me wash off real quick and I'll be right there." He smiled as Eric wriggled into his shorts and ran out, leaving the door wide open. If only life remained as easy as when you were little. Everything a new adventure, no fear of death or failure. No reason for modesty. He closed the door. There was something to learn from that.

He heard them singing as he approached the kitchen. He smiled. The two of them chanting along to the radio. Nice. He added his voice before rounding the corner. Eric sat on the counter. Todd grabbed him and threw him in the air then caught him. It was one of their favorite routines that always got a bout of giggles from the child.

"Watch out, you'll hit his head!" Reva warned.

"We do this all the time and so far, he's only had six stitches." Todd winked as he lowered a giggling Eric to the floor.

"He's just kidding, Ms. Reva. I had six stitches when I tried to climb the tree in the backyard and fell. Daddy didn't do it." Eric pulled up the hem of his shorts and showed the scar. A tiny white mark on his tanned leg.

"Oh, that's nothing!" She grinned. "It makes you look tough. Maybe I'll show you mine sometime."

Todd suppressed a frown as he thought how she might have obtained similar scars. The fact that she offered to show them interested him. He wasn't sure he wanted to see.

"You had stitches too?"

"Yes, a bit more than that." Reva pulled a paper towel from the roll by the sink and wiped down the counter.

"Then you must be *really* tough!" Eric said.

Reva stopped wiping and her shoulders stiffened.

"That's exactly what she is," Todd acknowledged. "And smart too if she can keep someone like you entertained all morning." He tousled Eric's wet locks.

Her shoulders fell and she commenced wiping again.

After a few tries, the ironed artwork lay on the counter for display. Todd and Reva had taken turns setting the color. They'd laid cheesecloth over each piece and pressed it. The heat soaked through the layer and supposedly sealed it, saving Eric's handprints for posterity. Todd salvaged Reva's shirt from the trash in order to press it. She barely protested. It was ruined anyway.

"Miss Reva, want to go with us to the monster truck show?" Eric asked.

Surprised, Todd shot a glance at the round eyes pleading him to give in. Todd had purchased the tickets online from the office before he left work. He'd mentioned it to Eric on the phone that morning. It was intended as a potential reward for behaving at Reva's house until he arrived.

"What?" She looked from boy to man.

"We have tickets to the Monster Mash at the convention center tonight. It's one of those truck things where they drive over cars and things. I bought them this morning." He wagged a finger at Eric. "There were conditions though and you know it."

"I already cleaned everything up." Eric held up his hands. As if he had recollected another requirement, he pressed his face into Reva's legs and wrapped his arms around her. She faltered a step to catch her balance and patted his back.

"Thank you, Miss Reva," he said.

Todd watched her face warm. Did he really see her eyes glisten? Yeah. Her eyes wandered from the painted shirts to Eric and then up to meet his gaze. *She gets it.*

"No, Eric. I have you to thank. I would have been bored to tears if you hadn't been here."

"Daddy?"

"Yeah?" He liked that Eric used the word even if it didn't rightfully apply.

"Reva can go now, right?"

Todd sighed. Damn, the kid liked to put him in awkward situations. Sure, she could go but did she want to? He raised his eyes to her.

"Yes, Eric," Reva answered for him. "Reva can go as long as your Dad doesn't mind—but you know it's not nice to do that. He may have already asked someone to go."

Seriously? Who would that be? It's not like he had time to socialize. In fact, he had intended to spend the night in front of the computer entrenched in invoicing until Eric called. Now, it seemed his weekend would be a lot more interesting and certainly a lot less tedious. "I called up Angelina Jolie but Brad answered the phone and squashed that plan. So, I guess you'll do."

"Well, that's a bummer. Second fiddle again." She grinned. "At least I know who the competition is." She whirled around and headed toward the door.

Competition? Did that mean something? Todd followed with Eric's hand clutched in his.

"I'll come by around six-thirty to get you." He scooted Eric out the door. "And Reva? Thanks for today. I can't believe she—" He stopped as he remembered his audience.

"She probably didn't know you weren't there."

Eric listened quietly. Todd didn't say what crossed his mind but knew Reva picked up on it. She nodded. *She knew; she just didn't care.*

"Thanks." He tugged Eric's hand and they headed home.

Man, she was something. The walk to his house was filled with Eric's incessant chatter. Eric held up the shirt and pointed out every paint smear. The kid obviously didn't get a lot of praise on a day-to-day basis. He craved it and Todd didn't mind. It frustrated him that Annie hadn't been the kind of mom this child deserved. The kind that would praise him for painting a T-shirt blue with his hands. Or the kind that would let him paint at all. As soon as they got home, Eric went to his room to put it back on and Todd changed into a clean shirt.

Tap. Tap. Tap. A knock at the door. As Todd went to answer it, he called to the back. "Eric, why don't you lay down for a short nap before we leave?"

"'Kay Dad."

He swung the door ajar and turned back...to Reva. She glanced around the room behind him.

"Hi." She hesitated, then reached a hand to his face. Her fingers were warm against his cheek. He smiled. "I just wanted to, um, do this." She entwined fingers into his hair. He couldn't help but stare as her tongue trailed across her lips. She stepped into him and pulled his head down.

What a unique sensation to have a woman kiss you when she's shaking so much she's practically vibrating. Todd wrapped his arms around her waist and held tight, trying to still her nerves. She relaxed. For a second. Then she pushed her other hand up to his chest, slipping her fingers under the shirt he'd recently donned.

Todd sucked in the smell of her hair and her skin. "Reva, you—"

"Shhh. Don't stop me while I'm on a roll," she mumbled.

He wanted to eat her up. She smelled delicious. She looked delicious. And wow, she felt it too. Reva skidded her mouth across his cheek and laced her tongue along the lobe of his ear before returning to his mouth and opening hers for him. He didn't hesitate. That tongue that had slipped so seductively across her mouth moments earlier, now tangled with his. A wet, silky dance performed together. It filled him with need. *Need.* He hadn't felt that in a while.

Todd pulled her from the threshold, his mouth locked to hers. He shifted Reva to one side and freed a hand to slip the door closed.

"You taste – amazing, Reva," he whispered huskily.

Amazing. Soft. Sexy. Sweet and incredibly female. Without thought, he grazed a hand up her spine and trailed his fingers through her hair. He reared his head back to watch the softness of it slip through his fingers before lowering to slip the shoulder of her shirt to the side. He nibbled at the silkiness of the revealed skin.

Reva moved her head to the side as if to give him more room. She closed her eyes and smiled. *She smiled.* The most seductive and beautiful smile he'd ever seen was focused on him. Then she brought those lips back to his.

"Back at ya," she said.

One more taste. *Mmmm.* Todd leaned toward her, lifting from the wall, straining to get closer.

"I'll see you later," she whispered. Reva trailed a hand across his cheek, pulled the door open, and slipped into the fresh air, leaving him wanting.

CHAPTER THIRTEEN

——— ———

Adam dwelled on simple communications too much. His ex had said it many times but he didn't listen. Not in those words exactly, but she had said a lot of things that he didn't care to remember. Too many, in fact.

He had followed Reva the night they'd had their first discussion. He'd done so mainly because he was certain she'd been lying about having a commitment after work. She'd gone straight home. Figures. Women are so dishonest. She just wanted to get rid of him.

He wondered how much of their conversation held any merit. Probably none.

He had decided to keep tabs going forward. His curiosity was out of whack. He wondered if the entire story of softball was pure fiction. "We'll just see about that," he had said the following night as he rumbled past her house around eight. The lights were off and her car sat idle in the driveway. He pulled past and parked two houses down, a step he had done the night before too.

His cell rang and he killed the engine, grumbling as it sputtered twice before going silent. "Adam," he barked.

"It's me." His ex-wife. Great. Haven't you taken enough?

"What do you want?"

"The car stopped working this week."

"Not my problem. You wanted it, you fix it."

"I know, I took it to the shop down the street. Remember

Bob, the mechanic? He looked at it." Yeah, he remembered Bob. She had a thing for the guy. "He said there was water in the gas tank. Sound familiar?"

He snickered. Yeah, he'd poured a gallon in but so what? "Nope, why are you calling me about it?"

"Apparently gasoline floats on top of water, so if you pour in several cups of it, the fuel pump will fill the fuel lines with water instead of gasoline and the car would have major problems. At least that's what Bob said."

"So?"

"So, did you or did you not put water in my gas tank?"

"Why the hell would I do that, Tina?" He hung up and didn't bother to cover a grin. It amused him that she was pissed.

From behind, he heard voices. Loud, boisterous voices. He glanced in the rearview and saw Reva and three guys headed down the street. They weren't going to her house, but on past. She had dirty shorts on and one of the guys carried a baseball bat and glove.

"Hmmm, maybe she is playing ball. And fraternizing with the entire team, it looks like. Figures."

He waited a while, then turned the key in the ignition. It took a moment for the truck to cough back to life, and he maneuvered it away from the curb. It tempted him to follow the group but he decided he'd skip that for now. Another time. Since she's so social with those guys, maybe she wouldn't mind if he dropped by some day.

He looked at the end of the 9mm he'd slipped under the seat. Maybe he'd go shoot a few rounds. Let out some steam.

CHAPTER FOURTEEN

Incredibly Loud, Super Fast, and Insanely Crazy – that's all Reva could say about the Monster Truck show. It captivated Eric and she couldn't help but be entranced as well. By the end of the evening she was exhausted and totally enthralled from watching Todd, Eric, the trucks, and all the craziness of the event. Mainly though, she just watched Todd. Covertly, of course. Sure, he'd caught her staring a few times; he just tossed a smile back and she went all mushy and hot inside.

When they walked out of the convention center, Todd grabbed her hand along with Eric's. The three of them walked together still feeling the roar of the engines in their guts. She attributed some of the rumble to the chilidogs and popcorn. The night wind caught them as they rounded a corner to head toward his truck. Reva shivered. This was *good*.

By the time they'd reached her house that night, Eric was fast asleep in the back seat, hunched over against the door.

"Tired. I'm hellaciously tired." She yawned and let her head drop against Todd's chest as he stood in front of her at the door of her house. A monumental step for someone who carefully measured every movement around her. He smelled so *good and warm*.

"Hold on a second," he murmured as he lifted his hands to her hair and fumbled. "You have some popcorn in your hair. There. Got it."

Reva inhaled the scent that emanated from his neck. So.

Incredibly. Yummy. She couldn't stop it, her mouth just had to go there. And it did. She touched her lips softly against his throat. She thought he groaned softly. She felt the rumble.

"You sure you want to do that?" he said.

"Come in with me." She opened the door and pulled his hand. An entire day of these two had her hormones in overdrive. Todd had lifted Eric easily to his shoulders to walk through the crowd. He'd dropped an arm casually across her shoulders periodically and she had felt the strength in it. He had no need to prove strength was there, it just was. He had no need to use it for any purpose other than to tighten the relationship between he and Eric, or perhaps steer her gently through the throng of people.

"I have Eric." Todd nodded toward the car.

She nearly *forgot about the child!* "You have Eric."

Todd ran his fingers into her hair, gathering it between a forefinger and thumb. He twisted it and watched in a trance. "I don't want to go," he murmured.

"But you have to. It's okay."

Todd pulled her to his chest and wrapped his big, thick, lift-anything arms around her. One of the perks of working with lawn and garden things obviously. "This has been the best day, Reva. I don't want it to end." He kissed her hair.

"I know. Me too." She slid her fingers up his back.

"There will be other days. Lots of them." He stroked her hair.

Would there? It had been a while since they were together. She registered the time since she'd seen him last and thought not. She wasn't the best catch and he didn't seem interested in anything too taxing. She understood that. Once burned, twice shy and all that. Admittedly, she had been a real piece of work.

"Like tomorrow for example. Unless something's changed, you still have a pile of rocks in the backyard that needs to be assembled into a fountain. Seems like that'd be a good project for a nice, sunny day like tomorrow's supposed to be. What about it?" He slipped a few fingers under her chin and lifted it so that she had no choice but to look at him. "Do you have plans already?"

Reva swallowed the knot in her throat, and shook her head.

He was so gentle, and big and tall and so totally *oozing with testosterone*. He focused over her head, staring into the dark, and squinted. His arm tightened against her back.

"Tell me about this guy, Reva. The one that put the fear of God in you and made you afraid to run on sidewalks or pass people and cars on the street. What happened? Where is he now?"

"I don't know really – how I ended up there, in that situation." She *really* didn't want to talk about it. He had already seen the crazy side of her family, now he wanted this too? No, he wouldn't want to know this about her. "I always thought I was a strong and capable woman. No one could take advantage of me. I could handle anything."

"You are, you know. You still are. I see it. You've had to make a few accommodations to adapt to what you learned, but you're still stronger than most. You left, didn't you?"

"I didn't have any choice. I can't believe I let it get that far. I hate vulnerabilities. I've always felt that if you prepare yourself adequately, you can deal with just about anything. I had no idea it was a contest of wills. He willed me to be the person who idolized and served his every need, even if I didn't know what need he wanted served on any given day. I willed to be loved as I was. I thought what I was – well I thought I was all that, you know. Unfortunately, what I was didn't seem all that loveable." She stared down at Todd's shirt.

"You realize that's what he wanted you to think. Don't you?"

She swallowed and shook her head.

"That's how he kept you with him. By making you believe you needed him—that there was something wrong with you. That you didn't deserve—"

"That I didn't deserve the nice place to live, the nice things he bought. The trips."

"Trips?"

"After the first time I disappointed him—the first time he had been angry at me for talking to one of his coworkers at a party, he took the dog leash and wrapped it around the neck of the puppy he'd given me. It was only six months old and I adored that dog. Nick pressed and pressed with the leash and watched me for a reaction. I don't think he had a clue what he was doing. It was like he'd completely disengaged from reality, he was so consumed with anger. The dog died right in front of me and he looked shocked at first that he'd done it. He apologized and cried. Hours later he told me that I'd better not think I could get attached to anyone else because he'd never let that happen. Afterward, he felt so bad he bought tickets to San Francisco and we flew up and spent the weekend on the wharf. It was romantic, beautiful, and so...tainted. He kept apologizing about the puppy and said he just didn't want to lose me."

Todd closed his eyes for a second, then drew them back down to her face. "I'm sorry you went through that. You didn't deserve it, Reva."

"But I did. I shouldn't have drank so much at the party and flirted with his friends. Sure it was harmless but it was still wrong. He had every right to be angry—"

Todd encircled her face with his strong, calloused palms and tilted her head upward. "Don't try to rationalize it. I understand your need to empathize with others and understand their actions. In this case, though, what you've just said is way off base. If you want to drink and have a good time, there's no harm in it. As long as you're not doing anything illegal, you're just enjoying yourself. Look at Tim and Ben. They have fun, but they never lay a hand on anyone."

Reva arched a brow.

"Okay, they laid a hand on me, but only because of what this guy did to you. They weren't going to let it happen again. I kind of admire that. And I'd bet my life that they'd never lay a hand on you, a girlfriend, a child, or a defenseless dog. Judging by what I've seen, I seriously doubt you did anything out of the norm with his friends."

"I teased them mercilessly. It was all in fun, but one of them said something a little inappropriate and that was it. Just like that. He lost it."

"And you're supposed to have control over what someone else said? Reva, your whole family likes to tease and have fun. There's nothing wrong with that. It's called 'enjoying life'. Just because someone else can't deal appropriately with it, doesn't make you responsible for their actions."

"Here we go again." She sighed.

"Huh? What does that mean?"

"You're acting like a counselor again."

"Oh, sorry. I guess it's in my nature. Okay, maybe not in my nature but you bring out that side of me for some reason. I just want to—"

"Fix me. You want to fix me. And you're so damn easy to talk to which is really, *really* distracting."

"Reva. You don't need fixing and that's sure as hell not what I'm doing here with you at the moment." He ran his fingers through his hair. "I need to ask you something."

Reva met his gaze.

"Do you think there's any chance that this guy would follow you here or try to stalk you?"

CHAPTER FIFTEEN

Todd registered the look in her eyes and knew it wasn't the first time the idea had crossed her mind. He hated to put it there himself but he needed to know the extent of the situation. The person sitting in the truck down the street in the dark seemed odd. There weren't any lights on at the house and no one else in the vehicle. The person just sat there, a dark silhouette against the glow of the streetlight beyond. As soon as she was safely inside, he intended to take a closer look.

"Of course not. My dad had him arrested for what he did. He wouldn't bother. Besides, I have a girlfriend there that calls every month or so. She told me he had already moved on to a new relationship. Another poor girl that will have the life beaten out of her and all her dreams crushed."

"That's a bit dramatic. You still have dreams, don't you? And you're definitely alive." He ran his hands down her back, spreading the big fingers in a fan across her waist. "Alive and beautiful in this light."

He looked over her head to monitor the person in the truck again. A hand lifted in the dark and adjusted the rearview mirror. *Was he watching them?*

"Look, Reva, it's late." Todd started. He wanted her inside. "I'm going to get Eric home and in bed but I'll be here in the morning. We'll be back, both of us. And we'll get that fountain installed. Okay?" He gave her a tremulous smile.

"Works for me."

"Good." He dropped a kiss on her lips before turning her to the door. "See you then."

Once the door clicked behind her, he turned and strode down the sidewalk. He faced the street, moved to the middle so there would be no mistaking his intention, and headed straight toward the figure sitting in the darkened truck.

"You there!" he shouted. "Get out of the truck."

The vehicle roared to life, choked out clouds of smoke, and squealed away. Todd stepped up the pace to get a look, but couldn't catch it before it turned the corner. Whoever it was, they *were* watching. Maybe not her, but someone on this street...and they didn't want to be seen doing it.

Todd rested his hands on his hips and watched the glow of the taillights disappear around the corner. Well, whoever it was, he intended to make his life a lot more difficult going forward. The beauty of neighborhoods like this—ones where they call the fire department when you're stuck in a tree and bring food to your door when you're hurt—these neighborhoods stick together and watch each other's back.

He looked at the front door of the house in front of him. "You have a teenage daughter, don't you?" he said to the air. "If someone was lurking around the neighborhood, you'd want to know." Todd stuck his hands in his pockets and whistled as he walked back to his sleeping son. *If it were my daughter, I'd want everyone to know.* He knew what he had to do. His mind was made up. He drove home, put Eric to sleep, and called Tim and Ben.

Adam had dozed for a second or two. When he looked up, there she was on the doorstep, with some guy. Geez, she had a steady stream of them around. They looked pretty intimate. He adjusted the mirror to improve his view. Did the guy see him? He sat still. Of course not, it was dark outside and his lights were off. *What are they doing?* He kept his eyes trained on the couple standing under the light on her porch. The glow of their bodies cast a single long shadow across the yard. Duh, he smirked, what else would they be doing? So, his prior assumption of her as a lonely spinster was off-base a little. Instead, she was more the opposite. How many guys had he seen around her house the past few days? Too many to remember them all. Ahhh. That's it. She's really into men, lots of men. That's her thing. She uses them, then casts them aside.

He tsked softly. He liked that she wasn't all prim and proper, had a dark side. She liked the chase. Made someone want her, then dumped them so that they wanted her more. Sort of an ego-thing, flitting from one guy to the next. She was the equivalent of a sexual harassment nightmare. She just kept it away from work. Or did she? Her actions toward him were subject for debate. Maybe not to that extreme but still— it reminded him of that movie, *Bad Bosses*.

Yeah, maybe she actually did make moves on him and he'd just read it wrong. He kind of liked that idea. Sure, it was a good way to excuse it all, or at least explain it. She didn't hate him – she *wanted* him. That's why she always looked down at his crotch when she spoke. He'd thought she meant to avoid looking at him or that he just plain bored her, but maybe not so. Okay, he could deal with that. Why wouldn't she want him, after all? He was more than decent looking and had been pretty successful at seducing one or two of the girls at work when he wanted to. In fact, compared to some of the guys he'd seen at her door, he was a damn male model.

Oh CRAP! The man was walking toward him, shouting something about getting out of the truck. No way. Adam turned the key. *Start, you piece of shit, start.* The truck grumbled to a roar and he shoved his foot on the gas. Did the guy see enough of him to know what he looked like? Had he read the license? The tires screeched a bit as Adam shot from the curb into the street and careened away.

Adam threw a glance over his shoulder. Where was Reva? Was she there too? *The guy is running after me? What the hell?*

He punched the gas, flew around the corner and sped out of sight. That was stupid, moron. Sitting around her house, watching like a stalker or something! Really?

Still, it had given him information on what to do next, and that was good.

CHAPTER SIXTEEN

——— ———

Reva's eyes popped open around 7 a.m. on Sunday. She heard voices—not the supernatural kind but *real* ones. They came from outside the house. She slid from the bed, tiptoed to the closet and grabbed her robe. This had always been a quiet neighborhood in the morning. Voices outside her house didn't make sense. She grabbed her softball bat from the bag and edged down the hallway. The sound came from the backyard. She tiptoed to the door to peek through the glass. Her shoulders bunched into knots as she listened to at least two definitely male voices mumble. She couldn't make out the words.

Sliding the curtain aside, she peered over the windowsill with the bat raised and ready.

She smiled. Todd's backside greeted her as he crouched to set rocks into place with Tim's help. *Nice way to start the day.* They had started on the fountain. Judging by the extent of completion, they'd been at it for a while.

"You boys had breakfast yet?" She slipped the bat down by the doorjamb and stepped outside. Todd stood and turned. His eyes traveled down to her open robe hanging off her shoulder, and the tank and shorts beneath it. The expression on his face heated instantly.

"Don't bother getting dressed on our account, Rev," Tim chastised. He scooped another rock and handed it toward Todd. Todd didn't budge. Instead, his eyes warmed Reva from the inside out, like an internal toaster. Tim shrugged and stepped behind him, shifting the rock into place. "Hello, the work's down here—you can stop drooling any minute now."

Reva stared right back at Todd. "Hungry?" she asked.

"Definitely." He grinned.

"What do you feel like? I don't have much."

Todd arched a brow and said nothing.

"Where's Eric?" She broke the tension and glanced around the yard.

"He's mixing cement in the front with Ben." Todd nodded toward the house.

As if on cue, she heard the boy's voice asking a million questions of her brother. They navigated a wheelbarrow around the various yard adornments and stopped short of Tim and Todd. Ben was no stranger to this type of thing, having done more than the normal amount of yard work with his own children.

Reva turned to the two new arrivals. "You guys look very much in your element right now. I'm surprised you didn't bring *your* crew along Ben."

"They're out shopping for school shoes right now. Benny blew a tire in gym this week." Poor kid named after his Dad and nicknamed Benny. They could at least call him Benjamin. Not to mention he was small for his age—not a good combination.

"Okay then, I'll make pancakes. It's the least I can do," she offered and stepped back inside.

Todd followed without hesitation. He glanced at the bat but said nothing, then ambled into the kitchen. He washed hands in the sink, dried them, and opened the fridge.

"Need something?" she asked.

"Thought I'd help." He stood in the room, one hand propped against the wall, looking big and burly and so completely sexy. He had focused on her mouth, then on the pebbles peeking through her shirt. "You distracted me."

"How so?" She paused with eggs in one hand and a box of pancake mix in the other. Focus somewhere else besides that big chunk of testosterone hogging all the air. Maybe out the window, or something? Look away. Now.

"Reva, I'm coming closer, okay?" He moved in. She didn't

back away. When his hand glazed her cheek, it didn't bother her. Not one bit. "Were you intending to use that bat?"

"If I had to, sure, but not on you. I heard voices outside."

Todd rested a thumb against her cheek and rubbed, while his fingers spread across the back of her neck. There was something incredibly personal and intimate in the simple gesture. And in his eyes, she saw something that hadn't been there before. It softened him and hardened him at the same time, as if they'd partnered against something. "Just us guys. No need to worry."

That was supposed to put her at ease? She wrestled her heartbeat back to normal and looked at the stove. "Easy for you to say. Um. You like pancakes, right? 'Cause I can do that or scrambled eggs. I don't have anything else."

"I like pancakes. Eric does too. Kiss me." Three simple sentences, two of which just sailed off his lips and past her ears. The third sentence brought her mind to a complete stop – heavy on the brakes. *Screech.*

"My brothers are right outside. Your son is—"

"Right outside too. So, you should feel ultra-safe right now. Three men out there to save you. Well, two and a half." He nodded at the wood by the door. "No reason to use the bat. They're all within earshot if needed."

Todd took the eggs and box from her hands, one by one, and placed them on the counter by the stove. He stroked a hand down her cheek then lower along her jaw and neck. The thud of her heartbeat rang heavily in her ears, blocking the voices outside. *What a fabulous way to start the day.* Todd lowered his head to hers, bringing it within inches, stopping a hair short of contact with his eyes locked on hers. He waited.

He slid his eyes toward the door and back. "The bat's right there if you'd rather have that."

"I'm okay. It's just—complicated. I'm complicated," Reva said, breathing his air. "Probably more than you need. You really think this is a wise idea?"

"Don't really care about what's wise, Reva. You're going to be okay. This is going to be okay. I've learned something about you. You're a lot stronger than you think. Come closer." He waited, and he stood there with that melt-me-to-the-bones mouth right in front of her. Holding. Breathing in her air, pulling her toward him. There wasn't anything she could do to resist. It had to happen. They both needed it. She put her mouth where he wanted it, right against those strong, wet, greedy lips that instantly sucked her into his world. *Mmmm. God, he tastes good.*

"Dad?" Eric had stepped through the door. He stopped when he saw Todd's arms around Reva and his mouth locked to hers. Reva struggled to pull back, realizing it must be awful for a child to see their father embracing someone other than his own mother.

"I'm sorry, Eric. Todd—your dad was just..." She had no idea how to finish the sentence.

Todd held Reva to him, not allowing her to pull away. The tightness of his arms felt good but the inability to move started panic rising. He recognized her concern and loosened his grip.

"What do you need, bud?" Todd asked. He seemed unconcerned with the situation.

"My cell phone was ringing. I left it on the porch in case Mom called." He held up the device with a small hand engulfed in a dirty work glove. "She wants to talk to you."

Reva broke free and moved to the stove. "I'll get started on that breakfast."

Todd took the phone and walked outside. The scowl on his face made it clear he had no desire to talk to the person on the other end. Reva watched him listen to the voice, his back tense but strong. He held the phone in one hand and the other hand rested on his hip. For some reason, that made her smile. Once he'd ended the call, he stayed outside a few minutes then came back in.

"Sorry about that. I said I wanted to help." He stood in the door, covered in cement dust, dirt, and sweat...and he looked—amazing.

"You are helping. You're making me a fountain."

"I meant with the breakfast." He dropped an arm from the doorjamb. A puff of dirt and dust fell from the sleeve of his shirt. Reva looked at the small cloud and smiled.

"I don't think you want to eat concrete pancakes, do you?" She raised a brow.

"I'll wash up first." He headed to the sink and turned on the tap.

"It's going to take more than tap water to get that out of your shirt. If you plan on helping, you need to—" Todd reached a hand behind his shoulder and tugged the shirt over his head. He wadded it in a ball and stepped to the door to toss the dusty fabric on the porch railing before returning. Her brothers cast a glance his way but they continued working.

Todd returned to the sink, took the soap and scrubbed his chest. Reva stared as small drips of water rolled down and attached to the fine hairs at his naval. She sighed seeing his back muscles flinch and roll with each fluid movement.

He turned and startled her. "You know, I'm beginning to see a pattern here. What is it about you and my shirts?" He grabbed the towel from the rod and rubbed his hands.

"I don't have a problem with your shirts. I just have a problem with dirt in my food. And for some reason, you always seem to have something on you. Paint. Dirt. Cement. Something." *Not to mention, I'm starting to like the view a little.*

"Reva, what do you need?" He put his tanned, hold-me-forever arms on his hips and waited.

What do I need? Let's start with those.

"Where's the griddle?" he added.

"Oh, uh. I just use a skillet. Bottom drawer on the right." She turned around to the counter and pulled a bowl from the cabinet. "Put it on the burner and turn it to medium. I'll have this mixed up in a second. Can you spray it with the can up there?" She avoided looking again as she pointed to the cabinet where her dry goods were stored. Once the batter was mixed, she slid next to him and used a spoon to ladle batter into the heated skillet.

Todd stood in front of the burner, his warm chest within inches of her arm. Suddenly Reva was very conscious of the fact she was still in her pajamas and apparently so was he - aware that was.

"You're going to get burned if you don't back up." Reva reached into the drawer by the stove and pulled out a spatula. She noted the bubbles rising. She raised the edge of the first pancake and leaned down to see if it had browned enough to turn. The simple move put her hair against his skin and she got a whiff of sweat, salt, and pure male sensuality all at once.

Todd lifted a hand and pushed the tickling hair up and tucked it behind her ear, holding it in place behind Reva's neck. "You're going to cook your hair." He pulled the twist tie from the pancake mix, then wrapped it around her locks in a makeshift ponytail.

She stood and met his gaze, which instantly went from amused to smoldering. He inched against her and lowered his mouth to her ear. "Don't worry, Reva, I can take a lot more heat than you can."

He pulled the spatula from her hand, slowly rubbing his fingers across the tops of hers. Then he flipped the pancakes one by one. After eons of silence, he transferred the perfectly cooked pancakes to a waiting plate. The tension was too much, too intense. Reva hated intense. Intense always ended up— more intense. She took the spoon and scooped more batter into the skillet for the next batch and in the process brushed it across his arm, leaving a large blotch of goo.

"Oh no. I'm sorry." She attempted to wipe it away with her hand, furiously working to clean the mess. "I didn't mean to."

Todd laughed. He took the batter she'd scooped from his arm into his palm. "It's fine, Reva. It's okay. I don't care."

"No, really. I'm sorry. I'll clean it up."

"Reva."

"Here, let me get a towel." She stepped back and tripped, sending more batter splattering on his leg and her thigh. She panicked.

"Reva, stop backing away. Don't you move a damn inch toward a towel, the sink, or anywhere else. It's okay. It's just batter. I don't care. Really. Here." He scooped the batter from his leg and wiped it—across her neck. Then he took the spoon from her hand and ran a finger across it, then wiped it on her nose. "Now we're even. Okay?"

Her mouth fell open and she looked from spoon to man, taking it all in. Was he joking with her? Taunting her with her own mistake rather than erupting at her incredible clumsiness? She had no idea how to react. There was a time when this was all she knew. Teasing and taunting with her family was common. Then it all changed.

"You did *not* just do that," she finally said.

"I did." He grinned. "What are you gonna do about it?" He baited her. *He baited her.* His eyes danced wickedly as he swayed the spoon over the skillet and dropped pancake dollops into the oiled heat. He had his back turned for a brief second and she took it all in. He wasn't mad. She'd gotten it all over him and he hadn't even scowled. She dipped a finger in the bowl of batter that he balanced in one hand. Scooping a finger full, she reached up and brushed it across his cheek. He swung around and she jumped back. Todd laughed. He shook his head and set the bowl down. He grabbed the finger and clasped it, watching her face as he pulled her closer. And closer. Oh God, she'd gone too far. She never knew when to stop. He bent his head and put the finger – in his mouth.

Reva practically salivated as he licked the batter. He didn't bother to wipe it from his face, leg, or arm but intently concentrated on her finger. Then he raised a brow as he leaned toward her neck, his eyes focused on hers. He opened his mouth slowly and moved closer. His lips were parted and she could see the moist tongue as it started a focused mission toward her neck. He was going to—

"Ahem. Are we cooking pancakes in here? Do I smell something burning?" Ben asked.

Reva stepped back and lifted the plate from the counter. "First batch is ready. Why don't you guys come in and have some. But leave the dirt outside please."

She dropped the plate on the table, gathered syrup, plates and utensils from the kitchen and stacked them alongside, then stood with hands on hips while Eric and her brothers made their way in.

Todd stood up, regained his composure and chuckled. "Saved by big brother. You are so lucky."

Thirty minutes later, Reva sat at her kitchen table with four shirtless men of varied ages as they gobbled the pancakes with fervor. She contemplated mixing another batch. They teased easily with each other. When a knock on the door interrupted their debate over who would win the Super Bowl this year,

Reva jumped. *Who would show up now?*

She opened the door to a petite, full-figured woman with stylish short-cropped hair that hugged perfectly against her face. The woman glanced her up and down in her pajamas and raised a brow. "You must be Reva," she said.

That one glance managed to make Reva uncomfortably aware that she needed more clothes, or at least not sleepwear. "Yes. Can I help you?"

"I want my son."

Oh. That explained the surliness.

"You're Eric's mother? That's great! Come in, they're all in the kitchen. Have you had breakfast? We have pancakes, or at least we did a second ago. Not sure now." Reva managed a smile and waved her in.

Todd stood and strode forward. He intercepted the woman as she stomped through to the kitchen. "Wow, you got here fast. I thought you said it'd be after lunch." He grinned. Obviously not the reception she wanted, the woman gave him her worst scowl. It was a doozy.

Annie stopped dead in her tracks. She looked from bare chest to bare chest then to Reva in her pajamas. "What the hell?"

"Don't go jumping to conclusions," Todd said.

"Conclusions? You're kidding me, right? A pajama party? Based on what's going on here, I think Eric needs to go home." She ran a look up and down Reva's attire. Reva pulled her robe tight around her shoulders.

"Well, that depends on what you think is going on. If hard work is a problem for you—as I remember from our past, it is. Eric has been helping us build a fountain in Reva's backyard." Todd sidled up next to Reva with his shoulder against her. Reva glanced down at the tanned fingers that rested against the back of her hand. "Reva, this is Annie, Eric's mother. Annie," he gestured with a hand, "Reva Zamora. The two gentlemen in the dining room are Reva's brothers, Tim and Ben. "

Reva forced a smile. "I think I'll go get dressed. Be right back."

"Yeah. Probably a good idea." The acid tone of Annie's voice followed her. Odd. Was that jealousy? Why? The woman had left him, not the other way around.

"Be nice," Todd admonished. Reva wanted to stay and hear the rest but her modesty got the best of her.

CHAPTER SEVENTEEN

———   ———

Adam had reached for his keys twice over the weekend for a quick drive-by at Reva's just to see what she was up to. He stopped himself. Now that he'd been spotted, he needed to wait and see how Monday went. Did she know he had been there? Had the guy seen him well enough to tell her and therefore report it? Every time a car's engine rumbled past, he stared out the window waiting for something to happen. Nothing did.

By one a.m. Monday morning, he'd let himself fall asleep. He was dead-tired and since nothing seemed out of the norm, he had to go to work as usual. She had a standing meeting on Monday mornings, so he didn't expect it to be uncomfortable the first hour or two. The rest would be the determination. Before departing, he decided to go into the garage and do a little target practice. After firing off a couple of rounds, Adam packed it away and left for work.

Monday mornings sucked. It was always dead quiet as everyone waited for Reva to return from her meeting and then vie for time to discuss their projects and issues with her. He himself liked it, mainly because, since she was unavailable, he often did whatever he chose.

Whatever he chose as in, let his curiosity wander. She had been right about him snooping on her computer. He'd never been one to back away from a challenge. Not to mention, when someone asked if he could help with something, he didn't think it right to say no because she hadn't given him explicit permission. Yes, she'd made it clear what his boundaries were, along with the boundaries for the other staff. He didn't see the point in restricting staff like him—ones with a desire to learn as much as possible. Reva had tried to rationalize it by saying her focus was on stability and securing the company's resources and data. Bullshit. She just didn't want anyone messing with her work. He had it all figured out. She was a control freak with a capital C and F. She liked that she had complete access and no one else did. Typical woman—had to have her thumb firmly in place on the entire thing. She always wanted to pull on the reins when a man was in full gallop. Yes, it had never been about the company. It was about her—and her ego.

He connected up to the new application server she had assigned to one of the other admins, and delved into the files. He had been curious about it from day one and, after their meeting last week where he'd heard how great it was going, he thought he'd take a look. See what he could learn...

CHAPTER EIGHTEEN

———   ———

Todd caught himself staring at Reva's roof again, only twenty minutes after he'd walked to the fence and looked over. He realized it was foolish but after the past few days, he had to admit his senses were on overload. He glanced at his watch. She must have stayed late again like she often did.

He had pulled a beer from the fridge, his first of the day, and held the can loosely in his hand. When the light in her kitchen flashed on, he experienced an unexpected sense of relief. He lifted the can to his lips and started to turn. The light from her window reflected off a shape in her yard—a moving shape. A man. Husky, medium height. Definitely male.

"What the fuck?" he muttered and slid open his back door. He padded across the grass barefoot, unsure whether to yell at the person or call the cops. He slipped his cell from his pocket contemplating what to do next. No one stands in someone's backyard in the dark for a good reason. He started to tap in the number on his cell right at the moment that it chimed into action.

At the sound of the ring, the shape on the other side of the fence jerked to attention, turned toward him and hesitated. He feared the person intended to do something crazy. For a moment, a chill went through him as the person reached behind his back. *Shit*. The man is dangerous. Seriously dangerous. Todd glanced at the phone display.

The sound of footsteps racing across her yard made him

look through the fence to see the person disappear around the corner of the house. *He's headed to the front door.* Todd ended the incoming call and dialed the police number.

Ring after Ring. No answer.

"Shit!" He ran into the house, yanked his keys from the counter, and ran to his car. He was in front of her door in less than a minute. It was the longest minute he'd known since he watched Annie walk out two years earlier. The phone had gone to a call center dispatch while he drove and he spoke to a voice on the other side that had him recite the address, phone number, and reason for the call over and over. He finally gave up and slammed the phone onto the dashboard.

For good measure and to wake up the neighbors, he honked several times before he retrieved the phone, stepped out and raced toward Reva's door. He had visually swept the street and saw no one. The intruder had left, hidden—or worse—was in the house.

He cursed himself for not getting one of his handguns from the case. He had hardly used them lately so it didn't register. He only had them because Annie had been concerned for their safety years ago. Since then he hadn't had a reason to arm up. Not until he walked up the drive and realized that it was quite possible that this peeping tom had been the ex.

In that case, the danger was significant for Reva and most likely anyone that walked in. For a second as he looked at her quiet house and the surrounding street, he thought maybe he'd imagined it. The very brief idea to walk away rushed through him, but he realized it wasn't possible to ignore what he'd seen. He'd never forgive himself if he left it alone. Left her alone. Like she'd been the entire time her ex brutalized her.

No, he'd not stand idly by. He called Ben as he loped up the stairs to her door and pounded on the frame.

"Reva, it's me, Todd. Open up!" he shouted.

He turned from the door and scoured the neighborhood as he waited. It was oddly quiet except for the sound of a vehicle sputtering to life on the adjacent street. Two dogs barked.

She opened the door partially and stared at him.

"Everything okay in there?"

"Of course, why?"

"I saw— Hey, can I come in or are you going to leave me standing out here?"

She stepped back from the door and allowed him to pass. He shut the door behind him and twisted the lock. Reva stood with crossed arms and drummed the fingers of one hand across her other elbow. "Explanation please?" she said. "I've had a long day and was just headed to soak in the tub when you tried to bash my door down. If I hadn't left my cell in the car, I would have dialed the police."

"Never do that again. It's not safe."

"Call the police? Ha, they're fairly inept at times but still all we have."

"No, that's not what I meant. Never leave your cell phone in the car. Keep it on you. All the time." She was in her pajamas and damn if that didn't get his motor running, even with the current situation. He shook it off and strode to the kitchen and dining area. He turned on the outside light and scanned the yard, then jogged through to her other rooms and checked each one. He'd never been in some of them and it surprised him to see how she kept her house. Neat but not.

The entire house appeared to be cleaned and then intentionally readjusted to make it just a little—off. Quirky.

Still, no trespassers. No one in the yard. When he returned to her living room, she raised a brow. "So, are you going to tell me what the emergency is, or do I guess?"

"There was a man in your yard rooting around."

Reva's eyes widened. She stepped to the door and looked out, searching for movement. "Really? I don't see anyone. How did you know?"

"I was watching out the window. I'd pulled a beer from the fridge and stepped outside and your light came on...I saw his shadow. My phone rang and he heard it and started moving toward the side of the house. Stay here. I'm going to check. Oh, and call the police." He tossed her his cell phone.

It wasn't the smartest idea to traipse around the house looking for a peeping tom or burglar. In one respect, Todd hoped it was the ex-boyfriend. He yearned for a chance to see the guy and make him pay for the agony he'd put Reva through. The man deserved to get a piece of his own medicine.

Although, if his college psychology course proved correct,

that's likely where it all started. Most abusers had suffered abuse and thus the cycle continued. He likely had already been through it so many times, the guy thought brutality was normal. How twisted was that? And sad, really.

As Todd realized the danger and the intruder had vanished, he shook his head and returned to Reva. She'd locked the door when he stepped outside and he had to knock again. When she released the lock and opened the door, he didn't miss the bat clutched in her palm. Nor did it seem appropriate to tease her this time. He understood.

Reva spouted off the address to a voice on the cell she had cradled on her shoulder, she motioned him in and slammed and locked the door after him. "I don't know. I didn't see him," she said to the voice, then sighed. "Here, let me hand the phone to the man who saw him. He's standing right here."

Some words were uttered on the other side of the conversation.

"No, he's my *neighbor*," she answered. Reva tossed the phone at him and went to the kitchen. She tugged a glass from the cabinet and filled it with tap water.

Todd gave the dispatcher the details. He hung up after a few minutes and a patrol car arrived an hour later. Good thing the trespasser was gone—he could have beaten her to death or robbed her blind while they waited. By the time the deputy knocked on the door, Todd had reached his limitation on patience. He flung the door open and started to growl, when the man spoke, "Sorry we're late, there was a head-on collision on the freeway. Really bad. Three teenagers in one car and a family with an infant in the other. Lost one in each. I hate coming up on accidents like that. Everyone's out having a good time and it just all changes in a flash. I had to work the scene until the emergency crew arrived."

Todd closed his mouth and blinked. The officer's hands shook as he pulled a pen from his pocket. Todd couldn't imagine what a day on the job for this man entailed but he knew it required every bit of civility and respect he could muster. "Thank you for helping us. Come in."

They perched on the sofa opposite the deputy. As Todd

explained his observation, Reva fidgeted. He reached out to cover her hands with his and squeezed. She stilled.

"And you're her neighbor," Officer Teckley stated.

"Yes," Todd answered, "and friend." He pulled Reva to his side and wrapped an arm around her shoulder.

"You're dating."

At the same time that Todd said yes, Reva vehemently stated, "No."

Teckley wrote something down, stuck his pen back in his shirt and surveyed the yard, front and back before getting in his car. He let them know he'd make a pass around the area and a patrol car would be in the neighborhood through the night.

Dating? He'd never really considered it, yet it didn't make him completely uncomfortable to say that. Still, it was awkward. Obviously, she hadn't wanted it labeled that way.

"Why did you tell him we're dating?"

He shuttered his eyes and looked at her. "Does it matter? It's better they think you have someone around all the time. That you're not alone. Or would you rather the whole world think you live by yourself and don't have a soul around to deter an intruder?"

"Oh, well, if you put it that way..."

"Besides, we've had two or three dates at least."

"Exactly when would that be?" she challenged.

"Well, you invited me to your family's barbecue."

"You and Eric. And that was just being friendly—not a date. I barely knew you."

"Yeah, but that didn't keep you from having your eyes on my butt most of the night, nor teasing with your family about our fictitious relationship."

Reva backed to the kitchen and planted herself on a stool by the counter. She rolled her eyes.

"Really? I didn't exactly force you to go and you started the teasing, not me. As far as my eyes are concerned, you weren't exactly blind either and I spent a lot of the time talking to everyone else."

"Okay, then there was the monster truck rally. And the baseball games." He ticked through all the times they'd been together, cursing the fact that his mind immediately jumped to the hot-as-hell kisses and touching.

"I don't think taking your kid to a monster truck show and pigging out on hot dogs, cotton candy, and nachos constitutes a date. The baseball games don't count – there's a million people there. Nothing date-ish about that."

She rolled her chair to the counter and effectively turned her back. Todd ran his fingers through his hair and clasped them behind his head. He moved toward the door, hesitated, then pivoted and strode toward Reva. With one hand, he twirled her chair to face him, then planted arms on the counter to trap her in. When his face was only inches from hers, he smiled.

"You can call it anything you want, honey. It doesn't matter. Tonight, though, I'm sleeping over."

He watched her adam's apple hiccup.

"No, you're not. I'm not—" She concentrated on the hem of her shorts.

"Right there." He pointed to the sofa. "I know what I saw and even if there's nothing here with us, I'm not comfortable leaving right now. Someone was out there in your yard. That doesn't bother you?"

"Of course it bothers me but that's not a license to—"

"Give me a break. I'm trying to help you Reva, not hurt you. Isn't it time you relaxed a little and let me try to do the right thing?"

"So, now you're a boy scout?" She meandered her eyes back to his face.

Okay, that made him laugh. No, he wasn't that great of a guy, but he wasn't the type she nearly married either. Surely she could see that.

"I'm definitely not that."

Maybe it was a good time to make her feel at ease and safe, but somehow safe wasn't all that appealing. In fact, safe sounded downright boring at the moment. She sat there braless in some soft tank top and shorts with a robe carelessly draped on her shoulders and expected him to be *a boy scout*? *Not happening.* He seemed to understand her need for taking things slow, but for Todd, even this was slower than he'd endured before. His body was definitely not cooperating with the knight in shining armor routine—not that he wanted that anyway.

Why else would he be watching her windows every night to see when she got home? It wasn't a brotherly thing, no sir. He already had a sister and she was a pain in the ass. It wasn't the least bit attractive to get stuck with another. Not to mention he had ventured beyond the friendly casual emotion somewhere around the time she gave him that hellaciously passionate kiss in front of her brothers. Nope, that memory and the nipples practically beckoning him under that top sent a whole different set of needs and desires churning. Unless he was completely stupid, she had the same urge.

He knotted his brow. *But,* and that was a big but, if he had to take it even slower to figure out who was in her yard and what they had planned, then he'd damn well do it. At least for now. He'd sleep on the couch and swallow his overactive desire to crawl into bed with her. He'd *do the right thing*...because that's what he did. What he'd always done.

ε ε ε ε ε

Reva lifted a hand and stroked it down his cheek. The day-old stubble felt rough and sexy. She had to admit, it was really a turn-on to know that he cared enough to notice someone skulking around in her backyard. He was so close she smelled the aftershave he'd donned that morning and the very male scent that was just—him. She sucked in a deep breath and leaned into him, placing a light kiss at the base of his neck. She trailed more kisses up to his earlobe and took a quick nip of skin.

"Probably not a good idea to start something like that right now, Reva. We're both a little stressed out at the moment."

She closed her eyes and slid her lips along his skin until she met his mouth. Her hand had dropped to his chest where she felt his breathing quicken. "Yes, you're right. Not a good time."

"Hey." He framed her face with his hands. "There are a lot of ways to relieve stress but this one is probably not in your best interest."

Reva huffed and stuck her fingers through his belt loops and yanked him into her. She pulled him close enough to slide legs along his hips and lock her knees to make him somewhat captive. To ensure he didn't get another boy scoutish urge, she ran her fingers up his back and dug in.

Todd's eyes popped up to meet hers. "I think I can decide for myself what's in my best interest. Question is, can you?"

She countered every move he tried to get back, to pull her arms down and away. Reva kept her mouth moving over him as he did. She hadn't been with a man in *that* way in a long time, and certainly not one that cared enough about her state of mind to hold back. It was a novel and very, very sexy trait.

"Reva, the couch." He stood, his body hard against hers. His hands running up and down her back made little circles and curves tracing sexy hot little tattoos on her skin.

"Couch is good." She pulled up on his shirt and started dropping feather kisses on his chest. He groaned.

"I meant—" he said.

"Yeah, I know." She pressed her breasts into him and felt the warmth of his skin on hers. Apparently that started the wall tumbling, because he rained kisses on her shoulder and neck. Todd bolstered her hips and carried her to the couch. Caution slowed him. He hesitated when his knees met the fabric of the cushions and dropped her legs to the floor. Reva sighed. Threading her fingers into his hair, she pressed into him and gave her lips over to another kiss. She opened her mouth and flicked her tongue against his, taunting him to join her. The feel of her hips pressed into his very healthy erection confirmed that he wasn't completely immune. She smiled, leveled her eyes on his, then turned him and pushed.

Todd lost his balance, fell backward into the cushions, and she dropped onto him. "Couch it is," she said.

Reva settled her smaller frame heavily into him and lowered to plant more kisses on Todd's chest, which had conveniently become barer by the second. She tugged his shirt over his head. He reached behind and yanked it the remainder then dropped it. She liked that he didn't force it, that she initiated the contact. Having control was a turn on, but his passivity was a problem. Had she misread the attraction? She ground against him. No, his body hadn't been immune even if he kept a tight lid on it. He had fought it enough in her mind. She wanted his passion, *needed* it. It had been long enough and painful enough. This was her time to blot out the past and find out what sex could be with someone that cared about mutual enjoyment. Cared about her. He did, didn't he? Why else had he watched and noticed the intruder?

It bothered her. She didn't need or want him to care about her. She had no reason to warrant it. She'd done nothing all that great. He was a successful business owner and a father of a terrific kid. She was what? The manager of a group of technical staff. The woman who ran out on a man that wanted to marry her?

Still, he looked at her like she was ice cream. She sat on top of him, fully clothed—well, okay, in her pajamas. She was covered. And his eyes said she was dessert. No one had looked at her like that before. Like he wanted to lick and close his eyes and revel in the taste.

"God, Reva. I don't understand it." His hand stroked up her arm and settled on her stomach with his thumb rested in her belly button. The feel started a tiny rolling, tumbling surge that settled a bit lower than his hand.

"Understand what?"

"How could anyone look at this beautiful skin and your gorgeous face and want to discolor it? You're—so perfect."

She sat still for a moment. No response came to mind.

"Perfect. That's rich." She snickered. "Just today, Adam told me I was a control freak. That if I'd trust someone and stop forcing my ways on him, he might surprise me."

"Who's Adam?"

"The guy I've told you about before. From work."

"Well, he's an idiot. You're as far from a control freak as possible. But if you feel like trying a little control on me right now," he raised an eyebrow and looked her up and down, "I promise I won't complain."

Reva laughed. She slipped a hand to the waistband of his pants and played with the tab on his zipper. She levered the tab down and flipped the button open above it which bared his torso. No underwear. That was interesting. Todd rolled his eyes and groaned. He reached his hands to her waist and pulled her down against him.

"Reva, you can force your ways on me all you want...but, I'm losing clothes left and right. It seems a little unfair."

"Unfair how?"

"To me. I'm half undressed and getting more so by the minute. God, I want to see you. Every inch of you that's been pressed against me the last few minutes teasing me." He slowly worked the sides of her tank up until it was gathered under her arms, teasing at the undersides of her breasts.

"I suppose that is a little unfair, isn't?" She grasped the fabric, yanked it over her head and tossed it. She worried that he'd notice the small roll at her waistline. This had always bothered Nick. *How can you work out like you do and have muscles that rival most men yet you can't get rid of that little area there. You need to rethink what you're doing.* Rethink? Yes, that's exactly what she had done. While he was in jail, she rethought her entire life and realized it needed to be lived elsewhere.

"Even more perfect than I imagined. Look at you." Todd's eyes were warm and admiring. *Than he'd imagined?* Without clothing to impede, he feathered a hand up her torso and cupped it lightly over the mound of her right breast. He teased at the browned tip for a moment with fingers that melted her. Reva wanted more. It had been way too long and his hands felt so good on her skin.

"You're looking at me like your favorite dessert," she whispered.

"Can't help it." He sat up, wrapped his arms around her and buried his face in her shoulder. His lips tickled and nipped along the skin then lowered to the softer area of her breasts. When he flicked his tongue over the very tip of her nipple, it elicited a groan that surprised even her. Damn. An overwhelming desire to feel more of it, to have more of him, urged her on. She tugged on the cloth at his hips, but her weight held it in place. She delved a hand inside the open zipper and Todd sucked in a sharp breath. His eyes seared into hers for a second then rolled closed.

"Still. Not. Fair. Honey." He dropped his head to her shoulder and didn't move while she stroked against him.

"Then show me how you want to even it up," she whispered in his ear.

That seemed to be the only encouragement required. Todd

pulled her hand free and eased to his back keeping his grasp on her skin as he urged her onto his stomach. He slid a hand down her small hip slipping it gently into the fabric. He cupped the curve of her bottom and held for a moment while his mouth searched for hers.

The kiss wasn't gentle or quick. He took her mouth and thrust his tongue inside, lunging for her response. She met him and for a moment their mouths stayed locked as the rhythm of his thrusting tongue tightened up the intensity. Her skin tingled from his hands as they stroked their way on her bottom, easing the fabric free. The tides had turned; and she had become almost void of clothing, yet his damn pants still tangled low around his hips.

She frowned.

"You trust me?" His words buzzed against her lips.

"I trust you."

"Good." He rolled her onto the floor and lowered above, balancing his weight on his forearms. He shoved a leg between her thighs to help keep his weight away; leaned down to plant another succulent, wet kiss on her lips. His pants dislodged and they were skin on skin, torso to torso. When he pressed against her, suddenly Reva hit clarity. This was it. They either forged forward or not.

Forward, definitely. The thud of her heartbeat pounded in her ears. *Wait.*

"Do you have a condom?" she breathed. She felt his heart against her chest as it mimicked hers. He sucked in air and stilled.

"Crap. Not with me. Hadn't really intended to be here, doing—this. I was trying to chase away a peeping tom, remember? I never dreamed I'd. Shit. This wasn't even a remote possibility at the time." Todd rolled to his back and left a hand lazily tracing circles on her stomach. His chest heaved up and down.

"You could go get one."

"I'm not leaving. He may still be out there."

"Then I could go get it if you tell me where to look."

"Yeah, there's an option. No. Not happening." He pulled his hand away. Reva wanted to cry. Or scream. *No, don't stop.*

"Then we don't?" she asked.

He leveled his eyes on her. "Guess not."

"Hmmm." She sat up and put a hand on his stomach. What a fine looking man. And now, he was backing off, doing the good guy routine again. Which *was* good. He was right. It couldn't go any farther. Not like this. "Okay. Get up and get your clothes on," she mumbled. He obliged.

Reva stood and pulled the tank over her head and shimmied it down to her waist. She tugged the pajama shorts up. Hands on her hips, she tapped her foot. She tapped. And tapped some more. "Nope," she said. "This isn't going to work. Come on."

Reva tugged his hand and pulled Todd out the back door, down the steps, and across the yard. "Boost me up." She stepped onto his knee, and waited for him to raise her over the fence.

"So, we're going to my house? You sure you want me lifting you up? The last time we tried this, it didn't end well."

"There's no tree involved so we should be good."

Todd laughed. She wasn't sure if his amusement was with the comment or her desperation to finish what they'd started. He bolstered her up and waited as Reva levered a leg over the fence and dropped to his lawn. "I'm good," she whispered.

He boosted himself over and dropped to Reva's side. Okay, back on track now. Reva was certain if they didn't get inside and finish this, she'd melt in a puddle of hormones right on the grass holding his hand. He tightened his grip on her fingers and practically ran with her into the house. Neither bothered to look back.

"For someone that's so concerned about *my* safety, you might take a few precautions yourself," Reva noted the unlocked door as she pushed through with his fingers doing that sexy, swirly thing on her lower back.

Todd flung the door closed and flipped the lock, then pressed Reva against it. "How's that?" he asked with his lips hard against hers. Reva answered by curving her legs to pillow his thighs and lifting up as his hands slid to cup her butt against him.

That's when Todd's foot hit the edge of the toy box that Eric left by the door and he grimaced as pain shot up his leg.

"Holy Mother of..." He tried to hop but her weight caught him off balance. Another flick of pain must have shot through his shin, because he dropped a hand to rub it. He tried to keep a good grasp on Reva with the other hand but she slipped. Down his thighs. Right down onto the carpet. Thud.

"Oh, man. I'm sorry. I—Eric's toys—I didn't mean that."

Todd reached down to gather Reva up. She glanced at his couch. Naw, too small. This'll work. One hand was lodged under her behind but she freed the other to reach up. And twist into the shirt that stretched over his chest. She gave a soft tug and he fell on top of her on the carpet.

"Oof. How bad did I squash you?" he huffed against her forehead.

Reva couldn't help but laugh. What a pair. Mister Klutz and Miss Clunker. Todd rose and bumped his head against the lamp by his chair. It crashed to the floor.

Reva clamped a hand over her mouth to stifle any further outbursts. It wasn't exactly the appropriate time for that. "So, where are they?" she whispered when she had gained control.

"Huh?"

"The condoms?"

"Oh." He bear-crawled away and disappeared for a few seconds then returned. "You sure about this?" He asked upon return.

"Very." *Damn, he's not changing his mind now?*

"Good. Then I just have one small request. Okay?" He hesitated. "I know it's more exciting here on the floor and all, and God, you look sexy—I just think we're likely to kill each other if we don't start out a little slower."

He is changing his mind. "Sure, I'm sorry. I'll just—um." She stood and smoothed her top down. Awkward. *Just reach for the door and go.* Reva stared at the doorknob.

"Oh, no you don't." Todd's arms slipped firmly around her waist and pulled her backward. "This way, girl. Not that."

"You said slower," Reva mumbled as she stepped back in a moonwalk, stumbling over his feet as he pulled her along the hallway.

"I didn't say stop. If we'd kept going at the rate we were, we'd probably need a trip to the hospital. Broken lamps, falling on the floor, busted kneecap. Here we are." Todd turned her to face his room. The soft glow of a lamp left long shadows across the dark brown sheets. He grinned. "Call me old-fashioned but a bed sounds a lot better than carpet-burn or broken glass in the ass."

"Oh."

"You sound disappointed."

Disappointed? Todd lifted Reva's tank and dispensed with it in seconds. He hooked his thumbs in the waist of the shorts and dropped them to the floor. An odd blanket of self-consciousness covered her as he stepped away and admired. "The only thing that disappoints me right now is how many times we've dropped our clothes and had interruptions."

Todd let Reva tug his shirt over his head again. When his arms caught, he grabbed a fistful of cloth and flung it. Likewise, he shucked his pants in record time. She would have liked to slow him down but the anticipation prevented it. They'd had all the disruptions needed for one night. This was almost like launching a space shuttle. Mission in sight, staff on board, time for launch.

She ran a hand down his torso until her fingers came in contact with the hard, heated length of him that pressed into her hip. Todd groaned. He captured her wrists as she started to move, then tossed her to the mattress. One knee firmly planted between her thighs and pressed against the very heat of her own waiting body, he trailed kisses from her neck to navel. She reached for him again but he dodged her fingers. Raising his own index finger to her nose, he wagged it and said, "No, you first."

Gulp. Really?

He lowered back to her belly and she felt hot air as he licked and blew over the skin. His veiled eyes glanced at her before he lowered that warmth further. All Reva could do was watch. Mesmerized. The tingle that trickled across her lower region and warmed from his touch made her want to smile back, but she didn't dare for fear he'd stop. She didn't move. Or at least she didn't intend to, but wow. He brushed his thumb across *there* and then followed it with his tongue. When he stroked again, she clutched into his shoulder and bit out a soft squeal.

She had to touch *him*. Surely he wanted her to? She pulled on his hair to bring him to her.

"Did I do that?" she asked. Todd glanced at the red marks where her fingers had clung moments earlier. He shrugged. She watched the shoulder muscles in his back roll as he dragged his body up until he could take her lips. He licked and sucked as intensely as he'd worked the rest of her. She melted her hips against his, completely aware of the very tip of his hardness pressed where his thumb and lips had been.

"Your turn," Reva whispered as she moved her legs to give room.

"In a minute." He settled in comfortably but didn't force it. "I wasn't finished. You weren't."

No, she wanted him to like this. It wasn't about her. She needed him to enjoy so she took control. She rolled over him and lowered her hips slowly.

"Wait." Todd sucked in a breath. "Not yet," he protested, but she ignored it. Reva slipped down further, until she had him completely engulfed inside. When his eyes rolled closed and he palmed her hips, she stroked again.

That was the moment he gave in. She felt it in the way he tugged her tighter and thrust to put their movements in synch. Yes, he liked it. *Her.* When he buried his face in her shoulder and blurted out a soft curse as he thrust again and again, his shoulders bunched along with the string of muscles down his back. Todd's body racked and quivered inside her as he came. Reva didn't stop moving until he let out an exhausted laugh and gripped her tightly. "I'm spent, honey. I'm spent."

CHAPTER NINETEEN

——— ———

Damned nosy neighbor. It's a fricking Peyton Place around her house with everyone always staring at the cars and people as they pass. Why had she wanted to live in a place like that? There's absolutely *no* privacy. Adam hadn't anticipated one of the neighbors would peer through the fence at her. The cell phone warned him of the person's presence. Had it happened a few seconds later, he would have been fully bathed in the light of her back window and therefore easily identified. Not that it mattered. He had no criminal background so seeing him wouldn't necessarily mean much.

Still, it angered him that so many people in her neighborhood had an inordinate amount of interest in each other. It had become impossible to meander past her house in the daylight. He shrugged as he waited at the drive-thru for his food to be delivered. He glanced at his watch. Nine p.m. She had worked late tonight. Obviously, she had no life. He grinned at the person in the window that passed his food out. Or maybe it hadn't been work. Adam remembered the body lock he'd seen her in with the dark-haired guy the other night.

It didn't make sense that someone who got that much action would be so difficult to get along with. So demanding. Normally, that made them more relaxed, not less. He grabbed some fries out of the bag and headed to his place. He mused that his habit of going by her house might be misconstrued by some. In truth, he'd never intended to keep going by, but he found it interesting. The first time it was just curiosity—a need to see what her life was like and perhaps better understand the way she treated him. Unfortunately, he saw nothing—not even her. So, he'd continued to drive by until he got a glimpse of her pulling mail from her mailbox. She hadn't even noticed him pass by within forty feet. So, he kept going. He kept watching. It was a bit like watching a car accident. You knew it was a bad thing and perhaps dangerous, yet you couldn't avert your eyes.

It was too pretty of a night to go home and a drive by Reva's was out of the question. Not with all her nosy neighbors. Adam coasted into Beason Park, near his home, around 9:40 and doused the headlights when he'd come to a full stop at the far edge. He left the stereo blaring with his favorite tune from Kenny Chesney. He leaned the seat back. The weather was a bit muggy and he rolled down the windows to defog the glass.

A tap on the back fender startled him and he swiveled around to view the intruder.

"You mind turning that down? It's too peaceful out here to listen to that crap."

"You don't like good music? Or just anti-American?" Adam had lost all patience and certainly hadn't the mood to deal with a complaining vagrant. "Go find a bench or something to lay on." He flittered his hand in a *get lost* gesture and slid the windows of the truck back up. The door jerked open and a small, fragile hand with inch-long red fingernails lunged in front. It turned the key in the ignition, pulled them out, then tossed them to the floor.

"Honey, I'm as American as it gets, but on a night like this I want to listen to the crickets or the locusts, not some asshole's radio. And I *never* hang out on the benches in this park, not even in the daylight."

He noted that the woman smelled like trees, and flowers. It seemed an odd combination.

He had ignored the voice, the hands, everything to that point. He'd written the girl off as a vagrant. When she pulled the door open, he was immobilized briefly by the shock of the action. When Adam regained his control, he bailed out of the car and attempted to tower his six foot height over the woman.

"You don't scare me," she said.

He noticed her hair was brown like Reva's, yet she had more of a mouth. She put one hand on her hip and rested the other one behind her in the waistband of her jeans. "Whatever you're doing here, you're up to no good. This is a nice park and we don't need any perverts hanging around. Now go on and get out of here."

"I'm no pervert."

CHAPTER TWENTY

The glittering spark of car lights caught Reva's attention as they shone through the side window of Todd's room. She was disoriented for a second then came to terms with the situation. An arm sprawled over her waist and the warmth of Todd's body snuggled against her back. The soft huff of his breathing tickled her neck.

She rolled to her back and he stirred. The bright light of the numbers on his clock told her that if she didn't get up and shower, she'd be late for work. Yet, the warmth of him against her invited laziness. "I need to go to work," she whispered.

Todd opened his eyes and leaned in to kiss her. "No problem."

She liked the way his hair arched up from his pillow and how the dark shadow of whiskers lined his face and chin. When his mouth touched hers, she felt the same excitement she'd felt when he massaged her skin the night before. Without thinking, she dropped a hand down his back and pulled his hips in against her. He groaned. "I'm getting mixed signals here. What you're doing and what you're saying don't exactly match up."

She smiled and shrugged. "Sorry."

Reva slipped out of Todd's bed. She pulled her pajamas back on, thankful that it was dark out and the neighbors wouldn't see her return.

"I'll drive you Reva." It was awkward. She sensed

hesitance. He tugged his jeans over his hips and fastened them.

"No, I can just hop back over the fence."

He pulled her to him and put a hand under her chin to lift her eyes to his. "Surely we don't need to sneak around like we're still in high school, do we?"

"Of course not, but I'm in my night clothes. I don't want people to see me like this and think—" She strung her fingers through the tangles in her hair.

"That we just slept together? Do you really think they care? Besides I don't think it'll shock anyone."

"I just want to go home without being seen."

"Without being seen or without being seen *with me*?"

"The first one. Look at me. I'm a mess."

"You're gorgeous. Drop dead gorgeous. If you want to go over the fence, fine, but I'm going with you."

"Why?"

"I want to walk through your place real quick just to be safe. Okay?"

She pulled her robe tight and waited while he slipped his t-shirt over the abs that had earlier warmed her back. A brief smile escaped her lips.

Later, in the office, Reva's thoughts continued to stray back to the night before and the change that occurred. She found herself forced to block it out and consciously focused on the projects meeting she had arranged on Adam's implementation. He had continuously refused to take advantage of the help of his team members so she'd taken the initiative and assigned two staff to him. The meeting would be their first. She wanted to jot down a few notes before they arrived.

With her head down and focused, the tap on the door startled her. She jerked up, realizing she had daydreamed again. Her eyes had glazed over as she pretended to focus on writing notes, but her thoughts had gone elsewhere. She had remembered her fingers sliding over the tiny scar on Todd's hip, a small white discoloration. She'd have to ask about that. She didn't know why but she had a newfound preoccupation with scars and their sources.

"Hey, are you okay this morning?"

Adam looked jumpy. He hung his head in the door but

seemed ready to run at the slightest need. "Yeah, sure. Why?"

"What's the meeting for? Is there a problem?" He looked over his shoulder at approaching voices.

"Not really. I just assigned some people to your team and wanted to meet to discuss the remainder of the project."

She registered the annoyance in his expression but there was something else too. It almost resembled—relief? That was strange. Reva shook her head.

"Okay, Good. See you in a bit." The sound of his footsteps on the carpet receded down the hall.

The meeting started late and went downhill from there. Adam had arrived twenty minutes after the arranged time. He apologized and stated that he had been in one of the executive's offices and it delayed him. A smug grin accompanied his announcement before he launched into a monologue as if the room had waited for his grand entrance. To Reva's annoyance, they had. She noted it as one more reason his project had gone nowhere while others progressed smoothly. Adam was easily sidetracked, wanted complete control of every detail, and didn't have the needed experience to delegate properly and control interruptions.

Adam announced to the new group members what he expected of them and why "he'd suggested" they be part of the group. *Really?* Reva frowned. When he stopped and took a drink from the Diet Coke he'd brought with him, Reva cleared her throat.

"So, let's get a few things clear before we move forward." She handed a stack of papers to each person. "These are copies of the project plan that we updated to include the division of responsibilities. I want everyone to understand that their part of this project is important to its success and staying within the timeline specified on the plan is necessary. You were invited to participate due to the large scope of the project and the need to delegate some of the responsibilities." She paused to look at each person. Perhaps she should clarify that it was not at Adam's request to include them, or that he had actually been rather defiant. Doing so would have been more accurate. And belittle Adam. As much as he deserved it, she suppressed the desire.

Adam took the opportunity to interrupt. "If anyone feels they can't meet the deadline or has issues with what they are requested to do, contact me immediately. As the lead for the project, I want to be aware of any conflicts or issues."

"As do I," Reva added. "I'd like to take that one step farther though. We will meet in my office every week until the project is complete. Be prepared by bringing your status updates with you. That should include a brief description of what was completed prior, what is left to do, and any hiccups or roadblocks that we need to be aware of."

"I'd like to see all of them the day before to review the content before we discuss them with Reva," Adam interjected.

That was enough. His desire to control what she heard and saw was evident in every word and action. It had to stop. "Adam, I appreciate that you want to be so thorough. However, this doesn't need to be that formal. I'd like everyone to submit the information directly to us in this meeting with no prior review or critique. We'll discuss it together and address issues. I don't want to stifle the flow of information nor accidentally leave something out."

Adam glared and shut his mouth. Reva noted the tight lines around his lips that signaled his frustration but ignored them. She delved into the papers that were handed out and the remainder of the meeting was spent discussing the project plan.

When Reva finally drove home that evening, she had a headache. Rubbing her temple, she noted the pain seemed to crawl up her forehead and nag at her. Not only had Adam been argumentative and disrespectful throughout the meeting, one of the team members had returned to discuss it that afternoon.

"I wasn't sure whether to tell you this or not," she had started, "but I think you should know that some of your staff are saying very negative things about you."

Reva hated the cowardice of people complaining behind her back but there was nothing she could do. The nature of gossip was that it was said without the target's knowledge—therefore the target had no recourse but to act with grace and ignore it.

"Really?"

"Yes, they're questioning your decisions on this project."

"Who's they?"

"I'd rather not say but he——"

"So, is it a *they* or a he? If it's only one person, that's a lot different than a group."

"Technically, *he* has said a lot of things to a group of staff, which I overheard. A great deal of them blaming and derogatory toward you."

Reva smiled and kept her composure. "There's nothing I can do about gossip. If the things you heard weren't directly said to me, it would be wrong to reprimand someone based on hearsay. Not to mention that, while I expect everyone to do their jobs with a good attitude, it's not possible to force someone to like me."

The woman eyed her suspiciously and rose to leave the room. "But he's making some pretty big accusations. I just thought you should be aware, that's all."

"What kind of accusations?"

"He inferred that you were delaying his project and interfering to the point of causing errors. That your plans were wrong and he had had to fix a lot of your mistakes."

Reva wanted to laugh. Isn't that what people commonly do when they can't accept their own responsibilities? "I believe a psychologist would call that transference...when a person transfers individual problems or issues onto someone else. Look, I am not going to get into the details on his project and discuss performance issues with another staff member. That's neither fair nor appropriate. Let's just say that mistakes were made and the steps we're taking now should correct them and get us started down the right path. I really appreciate you coming forward with this. Your loyalty is refreshing."

"It seemed wrong. Be careful and watch your back."

Reva had checked the shiver that crawled up her back. A few years ago, she might have marched to the gossipmonger's office and reprimanded him. Though his name had never been given, it seemed pretty obvious. It wasn't easy to hear this type of thing and not take it personally. She softened. "I really appreciate you telling me this. It was very considerate of you."

"I thought you needed to know."

"I did. And thanks." She had offered a smile to the employee, accepting the loyalty and kindness behind it.

Reva stood on her street and shook her head in frustration remembering the exchange. She opened her mailbox and removed the stack of envelopes and paper, and admitted the conversation had been awkward and stilted. The employee had wanted her to know more but seemed unwilling to give details.

She glanced through the mail one by one, then stopped at a single sheet of paper with a typed message. Even the feel of the paper seemed cold and threatening. Todd's footsteps caught her attention as he strode toward her.

"Hi there." He smiled and the troubles of the day melted somewhat. "Interesting mail?"

She nodded and passed the slip of paper to him.

CHAPTER TWENTY ONe

———   ———

Wouldn't you rather be at home eating dinner with a
hubby and kids than working late at the office?

What the hell? Todd's mouth dropped as he gazed at the
glaring words on the paper. So he had been right. Someone was
watching her. Not just the neighborhood like a burglar would,
but Reva.

Todd flipped the paper over to search for handwriting or
other marks. None. He frowned. "You know what this means,
right?"

She nodded. Her eyes were as big as marbles, the skin over
her cheeks paled instantly. "We need to call the police back."

Her hand shook as he engulfed her fingers in his larger ones.
She froze. Why would this happen now? Did she have a
magnet on her back that attracted this type? Had he decided to
follow her home after all? What had she done to deserve it all?

"Reva, planting yourself here in the street doesn't change it
or fix it. Let's go inside, okay?"

Except she didn't want to. It was safer outside in public
view. Bad things didn't happen there. They happened inside,
where no one could see or know. She looked around searching
for a face to associate to the note. The face she'd tried to leave
behind. He wasn't there, of course. There was an art to that
type of punishment. It had to be unexpected and unwitnessed.

"Um...want to fill me in on what you're looking for? An escape route maybe? Or someone in particular? I'm here, Reva. Right in front of you." The words jolted her attention back to him. He stroked her arm but she backed away. "We'll handle this, okay? He's not going to do this to you anymore. I swear it."

"You can't stop it. You don't know—"

"We can stop it and we will. You, me, the police, your family, your neighbors. You're not alone."

Across the street, Jeff from the baseball team jogged by and waved. "Hey, you two!"

Not alone.

Except, he had left the note to remind her just how alone she really was. And that he knew exactly where. The jackass hadn't counted on me, though. Todd put an arm on Reva's shoulder and guided her toward the house. "We're going to make that call to the police, then you're coming home with me. We'll call your family and let them know as well."

"No. It'll just make it worse."

He quirked a brow. "You really believe that? Or is that just something he told you to keep you from talking? Think about it. If you talk, he's exposed for what he is. If you don't, he can keep going. Putting you through hell. No, you were never meant to be quiet Reva. Sure, he beat it into you—but that's not who you are. And it's not who you need to be right now. We're telling everyone. You hear me. Everyone." He could almost feel the color return to her cheeks as he held her against his chest. The shaking stopped.

"Okay."

They made the calls. The police came and the curious neighbors peered out windows. A couple walked by to check on them. It was the second time a police vehicle had been in the neighborhood in a week, and that raised everyone's curiosity. Once the car had pulled away, Todd knocked on doors and spoke with each of her closest neighbors. By the end of the evening, it had traveled as far as three blocks. A neighborhood watch had been formed.

Reva's family was less calm. Two hours later, his small house was overflowing with people and a buzz of Spanish and

English. He had to really concentrate to understand what had been said, but somewhere in the mix he thought the brothers had decided to take turns at her house on the couch.

"She's staying here with me," Todd interjected.

A short family eruption followed the statement, before Reva's dad held up a hand. "No. Todd's right. He won't know to look here. If the boys stay at her place, he'll run into a big surprise if he even thinks about trying something."

"Good point," Ben added.

Todd frowned. It would be unlikely any predator who appeared at her door would make it out without a sound beating. "You call the police immediately if he shows, or you see anything. Understand?"

Ben ignored him. "Reva, you need anything from your house?"

"Pretty much everything but this is overkill, guys."

Todd recognized that she had spoken less than a handful of words while the family rambled away. Didn't they see the tension in her face? They all looked her direction.

Reva tossed her hair back and met their gaze. "I know how to deal with this. It's not that big of a deal."

"Not that big of a deal? Are you kidding me?" Todd barely managed to keep his voice controlled. "The man has already beaten you into the hospital and now he's sneaking around in your backyard watching you—not to mention that note. Reva, this is definitely a big deal. It's a huge one. Besides, even in normal circumstances, no one ever failed by being over-prepared for a situation."

He wanted to shake her. Instead, Todd pulled her to him and motioned for the others to leave. They'd all had their say. And had a plan.

"What's wrong?" he asked.

"I don't know. It just doesn't feel the same. Nick wouldn't do this."

"You probably never thought he'd hit you either when you met him. You thought he was better than that. Right?"

She quieted for a minute. "I wanted to believe it. To believe he was a good man."

"He probably wanted to believe it himself. And he wanted

others to also."

She pulled back and Todd lifted her chin. "So we take away his advantage and bring it all out into the daylight. Everyone knows and everyone watches. He's too much of a coward to come near you in that situation."

Reva put a hand to his chest and dammit if he didn't completely forget all the protective instincts and let his mind go back to the night before and the feel of that same hand stroking gently against his torso. Todd rubbed his eyes with a thumb and forefinger and forced the thought away. Or at least to the background. Was he really that messed up? The first thought he had was to get her back in the sheets?

"Why are you here, Todd? This is a big mess. Why would anyone want to be a part of it if they didn't have to? I don't have a choice—can't really run away it seems. You. You have options."

Did he? He supposed he could just walk away and let her figure it out on her own. And she would. Reva was smart and strong, even if she didn't see it. God knows he didn't really like or need the drama. Still, after all the crap he'd gone through with Annie, it had become obvious that as organized and devoted as he was with business—he'd never really put a lot of effort into a relationship. He thought he had but when you're with someone that doesn't really care about you, it's easy to just do what they ask and let things flow. To keep them happy. It's easy to believe that's how it should be. He had always been good at most things he tried, so it never occurred to him that more effort made it more satisfying. Other than with Eric, of course. Eric was worth the effort. Being his dad was the best thing he had. Until now.

"Most of the things that are worth having are worth working toward. Only the unimportant ones come easy, Reva, and that's usually because we don't care about the outcome."

She gave him a puzzled look and he realized he had spoken in tongues as far as she was concerned. But it made sense to him.

"And maybe the good ones sneak up on you just like the bad things do. It's hard to tell the difference."

CHAPTER TWENTY TWO

———   ———

Adam shook his head to clear the vision of matted bloody hair from his mind. *It shouldn't have gone like that.* He had just talked to the woman at the park and told her to leave him alone and mind her own business. He hadn't done anything wrong, just hiked up his music. Big Deal. Without warning, she'd lunged at him.

There had been no call for her to get all up-tight anyway. He'd been there before. She sat in the grass with a bag of bread at her side, tearing off bits and throwing them to the bevy of pigeons that surrounded her. He hated pigeons. They were nasty birds, good for nothing but making a mess. She crooned at them, and as the sun hit her back, he realized it was Reva. Reva was sitting there, throwing tidbits to the worthless crowd of worthless creatures, encouraging them to huddle around and waste time. Waste space. Make his life difficult.

He had no desire to see her at the park only minutes after he'd left work and expected to leave her behind also. The fact that she bothered with the pigeons made him bristle. Even more so when she shouted over her shoulder, "Turn that noise down!"

The music was good and lively. It filtered through the park and added joviality to the afternoon. He had no intention of turning it down. He hit the plus button on his volume and noted her glare as the sound grew.

Reva approached, the look of frustration evident in every

forceful step. "I said to turn it down, not up, you idiot. Can't you listen to the peacefulness of the park rather than that commercialized crap?"

Adam ignored her. She could order him around at work but she had no business following him to the park. Didn't she get it? He wasn't interested. She might be attracted to him, but as much as he considered it, there was just *no way*. Sure, she was pretty in a way. Yet, she was incredibly difficult to get along with. He stepped toward her with his normal forced smile.

"Reva, we have to quit meeting like this."

"Huh? Reva? Who's Reva?" The woman looked perplexed. She hesitated to step further toward him. "Are you okay, dude?"

Then, without his understanding, he looked down at her face covered with gravel from the park road and blood. Her hair was matted against her scalp and frothy with wine-colored shampoo. Only it wasn't shampoo that oozed from her head. He stared at the startled expression on her face. It had begun as surprise but now what lay their permanently embedded in her features was—forgiveness. Why? He didn't need her forgiveness. She was the one that followed him around, made his life miserable at work, then tried to seep into his off-time. As he stared longer, the features changed. It wasn't Reva. She was shorter and a bit plumper. Her hair, though now matted, was straighter.

What the hell?

"Unless this Nick guy has a way of transporting himself from one place to another quickly, he's not your peeping tom," Officer Teckley stated on the phone. "According to our investigator, he has been at work every day at his job in Florida. In the evenings, he's apparently joined a bowling league with his new girlfriend and, according to a neighbor, brings home a trophy almost once a month for some contest they've won...fairly consistently. Neighbor said he was obsessed with winning it. The guy's quite charming and handsome. The girl's a bit of a mouse though. Do me a favor, make a list of everyone that you've had an altercation with in the past month. Add to the list any new acquaintances that seemed random or odd. Email the list as soon as you get the chance, or you can fax it to the number on the card. We'll canvas the neighborhood again too."

He has a new girlfriend. A bit of a mouse. Go figure. Reva imagined that people had thought her a mouse too.

Reva measured the words with a solid amount of foreboding. Something in the back of her mind, said *think*. She had missed something. Something important—relevant. A coldness settled over her. *Think. How would this keep happening? What started it?*

She looked at the clock on her desk. She had officially stared at the computer screen for fifteen minutes without typing. Not one single keystroke. She hadn't taken her office phone off do-not disturb. Yet, from the flashing light, it was evident the messages had piled up. She hit the speaker button and typed in her code to hear them. Oddly, the first message recorded a time of three in the morning.

"Reva, Adam here. I'm not going to be in today. I've had a personal thing come up and I need to be off for a day to take care of it. Nothing critical, but it needs addressing. The project shouldn't be affected much. I can make it up over the weekend if needed. I'll take a day of vacation. Thanks."

Reva exhaled a sigh of relief. One less piece of drama to deal with; she had more than her quota. The remaining messages had come just in the last couple of hours during her morning meeting. No big crisis but a few things needed immediate attention and she dived in. The day surged by and when she looked up that afternoon, she was amazed that the time showed five-thirty and all the staff had left for the day.

"Hey." Todd smiled when she arrived.

Reva appreciated the comfort and warmth that came with the expression. "Hey back," she acknowledged.

He had waited on the steps of her house. He rose. When she walked toward the steps he dropped a kiss on her lips, light and warm. "Ready to go?"

They had agreed to leave her car at her house and walk to his. He had wanted them to go through the backyard to further hide her escape but she adamantly refused. It was overkill. This was a random incident, not a threat. Once everyone realized that, her life would get back to normal. She would stop hiding in Todd's spare room and her brothers would no longer take turns sleeping in her house. She would have all her things back in their normal places and not spread across an entire block. Todd would stop picking her socks from the living room floor, and her bag from the sofa only to position them neatly across her temporary bed in his spare room.

He had not understood the importance of these small but intentional bad habits. Habits that Nick refused to tolerate. Todd hadn't exactly liked them either but his method of dealing with it was less invasive and painful. Still, just letting the things *be* was important to Reva. He had not yet understood it. She disappointed him.

His fingers grazed hers as they strode up the drive to his house. It was a big thing to not pull back. He didn't understand that either. "I wanted to talk to you about the other night," Todd said.

"When the cops came?"

"Um, no. When we climbed the fence. I mean when we were here and things got..."

"Complicated. I know. I'm sorry. I shouldn't have—"

"No. That's not what I meant. I didn't want things to be like that. It was wrong."

Yes, she had expected that. The fact that he drew away as soon as things were done made her realize he hadn't been pleased. She had tried to make it good, had spent a lot of time and effort trying to stimulate him sexually. And she knew she had, judging by his reaction. Yet, he had immediately gotten up after climaxing and apologized. He had muttered something about it being wrong then too.

"I can do better. I *will* do better. I thought—"

"Better? You're kidding me, right?" He shot her a sideways glance.

"Why would I kid about something like that?"

"Reva, shit. I don't want it to be better. It was fantastic. It was—everything."

She opened her mouth to respond then closed it in confusion. "Everything," she repeated.

"Yeah, everything. For me at least." He stared at her.

Reva felt the heat reach her face. He was insinuating she hadn't liked it? She had finally been with someone that *wanted* to please her physically and it hadn't been good for *him*. "I wanted to..." she started.

"That's just it. I knew that much but it seemed like you weren't really acting on that. More like some robotic thing. You wanted to but stopped me."

"But I thought you were—" Yes, she had withdrawn when she thought he was finished and ready to rest. There was still a heat growing within her but she accepted that. She'd felt it before. He had not wanted to stop there. He had pushed to keep moving. It had confused and frustrated Reva. He was finished. Why did he continue kissing and stroking?

"I was. I did." He pulled her hands to his mouth. "But you didn't. That's not fair."

"Can we stop talking about this? This is way too personal. And would you quit picking up after me. I hate that." When he'd unlocked the door, Reva shoved it open and clipped straight to her temporary room. She clicked the door shut behind and set her laptop bag on the floor.

The door flung open behind her and she whirled around. *Damn. Forgot to lock the door. I'm slipping.*

"No, we can't stop talking about this. If you don't want me picking up your things, that's fine. I'll leave them." He shrugged and stepped into the room. Reva shrank against the wall, expecting more.

Todd dropped himself on the bed, his long legs extended in front and his hands linked in his lap. He stared at her.

Reva kept her hands in front, ready to move, and leaned against the wall. "I'm sorry things didn't work out as you hoped the other night. I'm not very good at all that, I guess."

"Is that what he told you?"

"No. I just figured it out."

"That's shit. Look, you're fantastic. This isn't about performance. If it were, you aced it." He grinned. "But I'm not grading." Todd ran a hand through his hair.

"Then I don't understand."

"Of course you don't. You were so concentrated on me I couldn't help but enjoy it. But I wanted you to also. Reva, that wasn't just about me. It never should be. Hasn't anyone every wanted to please *you?*" Todd stood and hooked his thumbs in his pockets. She struggled for a response but had none. He stepped out of the room and closed the door.

CHAPTER TWENTY THREE

———   ———

Adam surveyed his truck. It seemed fine. No worse for the wear. He'd get it detailed later in the day. For the most part, his scrubbing had done the trick. Fortunately, he'd been well out of the vehicle when she'd lunged so there was no need to clean the interior. Leaving her in the brush by the creek had been the only available hidden spot nearby. Based on the overgrowth, he doubted anyone had been that way in months.

Adam gassed it and headed home. The disbelief of what had transpired weighed heavy on his mind. *You could have just turned the music down, asshole,* he told himself. And of course he could have. But it was *Reva* and she had issued yet another of her multitude of orders. And expected him just to follow suit without question. Who did she think she was to make demands when he was on personal time? Not to mention that she had been completely inflexible with his project lately, forcing him to take on new staff and broaden the scope to include more testing and additional steps. She didn't trust him.

Then it wasn't Reva. It wasn't anyone at all. A random person that didn't like loud music and fed birds in a park. And he had pushed her. Hard. So hard that when she fell against the metal railing around the lot, blood had seeped through her hair within seconds.

"It hurts," she had muttered.

With no one around to call for help, he panicked.

Adam tried his cell but the battery had died and he'd left the charger at home. Hospital, his thoughts suggested. She wasn't breathing. She wasn't doing anything at all, just laid there with blood flowing into her hair. He loaded her into the back of the pickup and started toward the hospital.

The overgrown trail to the side of the park caught his attention as if it had been lit up just for him. He had weighed the scenarios available before turning down the path.

Now, surveying his cleanup job he felt the trembling hit his hands first. Then his legs started knocking and he lunged over in the grass of his backyard to empty his stomach.

Todd sprawled on the couch and flipped to the news. He often skipped local news in favor of the political channels and sports news. He grimaced. Much of the headlines were too disturbing. *Two shot in convenience store robbery attempt. Local mother of two and wildlife activist missing after night walk. Babysitter arrested after child found unconscious in car.* He sighed and changed the channel to sports.

Reva plopped down on the other end of the couch and tucked a bare foot under her. The white shorts accentuated her skin color. He couldn't help but steal a quick glance.

"Officer Teckley called today," she said. He waited. "He said Nick was at work the entire week and bowling with his new girlfriend on the weekend."

"So, they don't think it was him in your yard?"

"Not unless he knows how to time travel or has a clone."

"What do you think?" Todd asked.

"I'm not sure. I guess I never really thought it was him. Something wasn't right. If it *had* been, I think he'd want me to know he'd been there. He would have done something to signal that he knew where I was. He liked to instill fear as much as he liked to instill pain."

"You mean he'd taunt you?"

"Yeah, pretty much."

"What a sick fuck."

She stared at the glass of water in her hand and nodded. "You have no idea." She swirled the water and continued to watch it slosh. Todd knew there was more she wanted to tell him. He waited. The sofa bounced as she turned toward him and pulled the other leg underneath her bottom.

"The answer to your question is no. Not the way you're talking about."

"Just so we're on the same page, do you want to expand on that? What are we talking about now?"

"You asked if he'd wanted to please me. That's a no."

"Technically, I asked if anyone wanted to—not him. I wasn't sure if we were talking about Teckley's call or well...that. Listen, did Teckley have any idea who it was?" He knew she wanted to talk about the other thing more, but it wasn't near as important. And for some reason, his stomach turned at the thought of such a relationship. Knowing who this person was, and why they were after her seemed a bit more critical. Especially if there was a potential for harm.

"Oh, um...no, he said they were going to interview the neighbors and he asked me to make lists of people I'd had altercations with or who seemed odd or new."

"Am I on that list?"

Her eyes flew to his. "Of course not. Why'd you ask that?"

"Well, I'm new. We've only known each other a short while."

She frowned. "Are you trying to confuse me?"

He grinned. "So, you don't consider me dangerous then?"

She lifted off her knees and crawled toward him, launching against his chest. His breath let out in a whoosh.

"Dangerous? Possibly. Stalker or Peeping Tom?" She glanced down his length. "I fail to see why you'd need to resort to that, under the circumstances. You seem more than capable of having a normal relationship without resorting to hiding or following people."

"A normal relationship," he repeated. Todd slipped his hands behind her and locked them around Reva's waist. "You mean one that *two* people choose to be in because it's mutually enjoyable."

"Something like that."

"I haven't got a clue what that is," he teased.

"Me either."

A loud rap on the door startled them. Todd was about to just call out for them to come in but he remembered he'd started locking it when Reva arrived. He ignored the knock and pulled her up to his lips so he could brush a kiss on hers. A soft thump signaled whoever had knocked was still waiting. The rasp of a key entering the doorknob caught his attention. His dropped the hand that had grazed up Reva's back and lifted her off.

"Go to the back," Todd ordered.

"But—"

"Go! I'll be there in a min—" The door flew open.

"Hi Dad." Eric smiled. His small face moved from Reva to Todd. "Hi, Ms. Reva."

"Hey, bud." Todd looked past him at the car pulling away from the drive. "What are you doing here?"

"Mom had to go on an overnight business thing. She said you were going to take me rock climbing at the park."

Todd squelched the frown, but clenched a hand around Reva's wrist so she wouldn't remove herself from the room. Damn Annie. No call, nothing. And she didn't even check to see if he was home! Or that he had company.

"Okay, well I don't know about rock climbing but come on in." He reached for the bag. "You're gonna have to share with me though because Reva's in your room right now."

"Really? So you *did* move in with us? That's great!" His eyes swiveled from Todd to Reva. "Dad, why doesn't she have to share? It's *my* room."

Reva laughed. "He has a point, you know."

Todd shifted the bag to his other arm and let go of her. "Well, that'd only mean one thing, you know."

She shook her head. "Nope. That's not happening."

He grinned. "I sleep on the couch." It probably wasn't a good idea to remind her that they'd made good use of his bed already. Not with Eric present.

Reva's mouth dropped. "Oh, I thought you meant..."

"What? That I'd share a room with you when I hardly know you? What would your mom and dad say?" he teased. But he did know her. Every soft, silky inch and he craved them all.

Reva punched Todd in the arm and went to her/Eric's room. "I'll take the couch," she shot over her shoulder, "but I'm sharing a bathroom with somebody. You guys decide."

"Okay." Todd heaved a fake sigh. "I guess I'll let you use

mine."

Reva dragged her bag of clothes and toiletries out to the living room and dumped it against a wall. Todd watched as she neatly laid open the lid and surveyed the contents. "You can put those in the back room, if you want to."

Sure, it was his room too, but she obviously had a hang-up about Eric seeing them together.

"This is fine."

"And makes the room look like a college dorm. Come on, Eric. Let's see what we can find to eat." He pulled Eric into the kitchen and they rummaged through the fridge.

"Do you want me to move it?" she called after them.

He didn't really care. If he were expecting company maybe, but—she *is* company. "It doesn't matter. Put it wherever you want."

A few minutes later, she joined them in the kitchen. They made dinner and ate. It was the first time Todd had had a woman at the dinner table since Annie left. Not that he hated cooking or specifically cooking for a woman, it just never happened. He didn't invite women home as a habit. He hadn't been celibate either—it just never appealed to come here. Now, he had a scarred but enticing woman at his table, and her make-up was tucked into a corner of his bathroom. After Annie, that should scare him to death, but it hadn't. Admittedly, it was a strange but welcome feeling.

Her news had confounded him too. He thoroughly expected the ex to be the stalker. As gorgeous as she was, he doubted any man would give up easily. Yet, if Agent Teckley's report was accurate, and it must be, Nick had been ruled out. They were stumped. No other likely candidate had surfaced from the neighborhood either, or Teckley wouldn't have asked Reva for that list of names. Still, and for the life of him he didn't know why, he wanted to validate the guy's whereabouts.

"Time for bed, Eric." Todd roused the boy from his half-sleep on the floor. Eric had constructed some sort of war game from a collage of various pieces of plastic in a box by the table. Once satisfied with the result, he'd simply settled right in the middle of it and surveyed his territory. His tiny eyelashes bobbled up and down in a fight to keep his eyes open. Todd lifted him, cradled the tiny frame over his shoulder and stepped across the construction toward the back rooms.

CHAPTER TWENTY FOUR

——— ———

Todd frowned at his computer screen. They had an order for ten of the fountains he'd tested from a big hardware store chain. Good news financially. Unfortunately, they'd just discovered the bottom sections leak and water tended to seep from them. He'd been on the phone with the vendor a couple of times but they were unresponsive. Filling the order would probably end up in returned merchandise and a loss if they didn't straighten it out. He sighed. Another small disruption that compounded all the other things going on.

At what point were you going to tell me that you were living with someone? Annie was pissed. What business was it of hers anyway? She had been screwing around on him after the second year of marriage. Who was she to judge? Last he checked, he was still single, thanks to her. He had told her as much. Just before she dropped the ball that hammered home the control she still had on his life. A reminder that he'd merely imagined he had rid himself of her.

"Todd, that's not the kind of environment I want Eric exposed to. He needs stability. Not women running in and out of your bedroom at your whim." That was like the pot calling the kettle...

"Stability, Annie?" He controlled his voice, but the severity in tone made it impossible to hide his contempt. "You dump him on me without even calling half the time, and flit off on your next adventure with your *married* boyfriend. When you're gone, you don't call and, frankly, I doubt you give a shit what's going on with him as long as you get your fling out of your system. There is *nothing* stable in this boy's life right now *except* me. I am here—whenever he comes, no matter what, no matter when. Don't you dare condemn me for helping Reva out of a bad situation. She's not running in and out of my bed on a whim. But she's damned well here, and if you don't like it, you can just go fuck yourself, for all I care."

Silence had fallen over the phone and he heard the sound of voices in the background. It occurred to him that she was out enjoying herself while chastising him. The irony of the situation angered him further.

"Well, I just don't think Eric should get too attached when she might be gone in a week. Maybe he shouldn't come around there for a while until you get your life straightened out."

"Get *my* life straightened out? You have to be kidding me. There's nothing to straighten out, Annie. I love Eric. I'm here for him. Reva's a friend and I care about her too. She has something really bad going on and we're helping her through it. She's not going to be gone in a week." He had ended the call to ensure he didn't say worse.

He pondered that statement further as he sifted through the emails about his fountain order. Truth was, he didn't know if she'd be gone in a week or even a day. And he had no idea if he wanted her to stay anyway. She was only there until they caught the person bothering her. He hadn't thought about what might happen if they didn't. It was hard not to think about her as he worked. The sex had been pretty damned awesome even though she was inordinately obsessed with his satisfaction over her own. But he didn't want a relationship and she definitely didn't either. She'd had her fill of men. And since she'd been in his house, she'd barely come near him.

That was a good thing, right?

More irony hit him. No, it wasn't. *And why the hell not?* He realized Annie's entire life revolved around controlling and manipulating the men around her. Reluctantly, he admitted that she still pulled his strings. Reva hadn't made any effort at all to do so, yet here he was, fantasizing about her. He had some undefined need to get rid of the asshole bothering her too. For the life of him, he didn't know why he needed it. Or cared. Male ego maybe? Protective instincts?

The phone rang and rang, yet he didn't attempt to pick up. He didn't have the stomach for more intense discussions with customers at the moment. One of the others would get it. He threw a pen across the desk. Damn. Both of these women were so entrenched in his thoughts at the moment that he'd taken his mind off work and had accomplished nothing all morning. Dammit. This was *not* going to happen. He had a business to run; he didn't have time to idle away precious minutes on a woman. Correction...women.

"Annie can go to hell for all I care," he muttered. Still, the woman had threatened to cut off his contact with Eric. In fact, she'd flat out said he wasn't coming over again until Reva was gone. How dare she throw ultimatums at him? And Reva. She'd settled into his living room and become extraordinarily nice and complacent. Distant. Like a damn valet or something. He wanted the woman that had made him boost the fence. That's the real girl. Not this cardboard cutout that avoided contact. "And Reva too."

But he didn't mean it.

Todd slammed the door when he arrived from work, jolting Reva's attention from her review of the new project she had worked on at his coffee table for the past two hours. She glanced at the time on the screen. Five after eight; he'd obviously had less than a stellar day. She cocked an eyebrow when he tossed keys on the kitchen counter and strode past her to the bedroom. He hadn't glanced her way and when the door closed decisively, she took that as a *leave me alone* gesture. She shrugged. As long as he stayed there, she wouldn't get worried.

He didn't.

Bare-chested and in loose fitting shorts, he strode through the room. He grabbed beer from the fridge and exited to the backyard. She watched through the window as he took two drags from the beer and plopped it on the table, then went to a garden shed in the back corner. He came out with a bunch of tools. He hacked at the bushes along the side fence as if they were insurgents attacking his castle. The fierce movements rippled through his shoulders and back.

The glisten of sweat showed on his forearms before Reva realized she'd stared out the window for at least twenty minutes. She knew better than to interrupt a man on a mission and he certainly seemed to be. Yet, the anger seemed to drive his actions more than anything else. If she didn't at least *ask,* she was certain the bush would be nothing but a six-inch stalk before he was done.

"Todd, you want a drink of ice tea?" She held out the glass and smiled. He swung his eyes to her. Cold. Hard. Whatever was going on, he was filled with it.

"Thanks. I have a beer," he said through tight lips.

She waited while he went to his beer and took three long sips, his eyes slivered through dark lashes at her. She reassessed the intention to ask what was wrong. She'd learned a long time ago not to pry. Besides, she wasn't sure she wanted to know.

"You don't want that bush anymore?"

He slid eyes to the leaves and seemed to wake up. The previously five-foot tall leafy life was at mid-thigh and diminishing. The weight of the world almost visually slid from his shoulders onto the pile of debris at their feet. Todd gave a short laugh. "I guess I got a little carried away."

"Did you? I thought maybe you wanted to get rid of it entirely." She recognized the symbolism in her words. *Get rid of it entirely. Get rid of me entirely.* All he had to do was say so. Maybe it was time to go home. Whatever her threat was, whoever it was. They're gone now.

Todd grabbed the glass from her fingers and drank it down in one long effort. "No. Just trim it back a bit. It was starting to peek through the fence." He handed the glass back to her, the touch of his fingers along hers warm and wet with sweat. "If it twines itself into the fence, the boards will start loosening and fall off. Eventually, they'd be destroyed and I'd have to replace them."

God, did he really intend the analogy of it all? Was she really intruding on his life that much? Entwining herself into his home, his life, until he needed to extricate her before things got completely awkward?

"Um. I was thinking I should probably go home this weekend. Things seem to have calmed down."

The fact that it startled him into looking at her again left a small tingle of warmth. "Annie is refusing to let me see Eric as long as you're here," he stated flatly.

Well that seals it. "I'll get my things together and head home tonight then."

"NO."

"Yes, I don't want to cause problems. You've been great. Besides, whoever it was is gone."

"That's a bad idea." His words didn't match the gruffness in his voice. Nor the abrupt, severe movements he made as he lifted the shears and strode to deposit them in the shed. He reappeared a minute later and practically mowed her down as he lifted the pile of green flitters and carried them to the trash. Reva stepped back and folded her hands across her chest with the glass in hand.

"You're angry," she stated.

"Yesss. Why do women have to control every miniscule thing? What the hell is wrong with just letting a person enjoy themselves and not intrude on it? Tell me, Reva. Is that like a training thing women go through as teenagers or something? They think they have to dangle themselves like carrots in front of a guy just waiting for him to try to grab it, then jerk the damn thing away? And like idiots, we grab and think there's something worth the effort in there. But there isn't."

Reva gulped and blinked. "I don't..." She was confused.

"That's right. You don't. I do, and I keep thinking it's *worth it*. But it's not. I'm sick of it. I don't need this shit. I have a business to run. And whether she knows it or not, I'm the best damn parent Eric has right now. Why does there always have to be some stupid drama?"

"Yes, you are." She didn't look away. "Which is why I need to leave. He needs you."

He tossed the last of the leaves into the trash and brushed his hands together. Reva was keenly aware of the muscles in his chest heaving up and down. Todd stomped toward her. "What *exactly* do *you* need, Reva? Have you ever considered that?"

"I don't need anything."

"Then what the hell do you *want*?" He turned to his beer and threw back the last of the liquid that must have been hot after sitting so long.

"Nothing." The smell of the cut leaves wafted around them. A sweet accent to the sour air. She moved from one leg to the other and looked over the fence at her yard. "I'll go now."

Squaring her shoulders, Reva lifted bare feet and moved to his back door. She slid the glass open and tufted across the carpet to her bag. She'd just take what she could carry and send one of her brothers for the rest. Tim was at the house now. He could gather it all up.

"No." Todd's voice feathered lightly against her ear.

"It's best. For you."

"It's not Reva, and I'll be the one to decide what's best for me."

"I'm not trying to—" She wanted to say *control you,* but Todd grabbed her arms.

He pulled her against him, turning her body to curl into his chest. His rock solid, sweaty and slick chest. *Mmmm.* Damn, it was hard not to want to stroke that, even with all the anger burning underneath. Unfortunately, he'd made it very clear that he'd had enough women in his life. *I don't need this shit,* he'd said. Well, neither did she.

She wrenched her hands up against his skin and pushed hard. He tightened his grip.

"You're staying. If you leave, she wins again. This isn't something she has any say in. I won't let her. Yeah, Eric needs me. And I need him. But I'll be damned if that woman is going to push my buttons again."

"I don't *want* to stay. I want to *go home.* I want to get back to *normal.*"

Todd lowered his head closer and stared at her mouth. "Tell me something," he murmured against her lips, "what's so great about normal?"

No answer was expected. He brushed his lips across hers. Once. Twice. Then glanced across her nose before delving his tongue into parted lips that waited for him.

Good tonsils, she thought. Warm, wet kisses. Scratch that. These were hot, wet kisses that he rained on her hungrily. His anger had simmered much of the day and though it had eased, there were still flames of emotion firing his desire. What's great about normal? She knew she didn't want the life she had with Nick. Nor did she want whatever was happening now. Okay, well *now at this moment* was *good.*

Todd engulfed her in sweat, testosterone, and his delicious male scent. Whatever the emotion he'd had earlier appeared to have slipped from between them and propelled him into her. He kissed hard, seeking to dig into her. To whittle away at the control she'd had thus far. Maybe the control didn't matter. What good had it done her? The life she'd had certainly had no strings of normalcy. Maybe normal *was* overrated. Maybe anything more than just this was too. She knew he was sick of it. Sick of women. Sick of her. But this felt like the first *real* good thing she'd wanted in years. And she did want it. Him. But it scared her.

Uh-oh.

CHAPTER TWENTY FIVE

——— ———

Epiphanies come at the strangest, most inconvenient moments. Todd frowned at Reva unintentionally. Her eyes were open, not closed as a man would expect from a woman. Her mouth warm and inviting. *She wanted to leave*, but for all the wrong reasons. In fact, he doubted it was what she wanted at all. He had no false impression she wanted to be with him. No, the clarity of what she'd been through had to make her realize the importance of family and friends in the situation. His house was simply safer. Still, with his announcement about Annie's ultimatum, she'd take the risk. She'd leave.

But *he* wanted her to stay.

"What?" Reva's brows furrowed.

"Tomorrow's Friday, right?"

"All day, why?"

"Annie told Eric I'd take him rock climbing." He ran a hand over Reva's hair.

"So, you're taking him tomorrow? Don't you think he's a little young for that?"

Todd smiled. "No. I thought I'd take him Saturday. There's a park about an hour off the freeway that has several large granite outcroppings. It's more of a nature trail but since it's all rocky, we call it rock climbing."

"I know the place. I've been there."

"You stay two more days and we'll all get up in the morning and go. It'll be nice. We can pack a lunch and eat it when we get to the top. Eric loves the place."

"Uh, that's kind of a bad idea, under the circumstances."

"What circumstances?"

"Annie doesn't want me here—or around Eric."

"Annie doesn't get to vote."

"She said—"

"She also promised I'd take Eric rock climbing when she dropped him off last weekend. She wouldn't dare back out. She can't possibly refuse since she's the one that suggested we go. Why waste it?" He patted her cheek and extracted himself from her grip. Or released her from his.

Reva agreed reluctantly. Friday evening though, he debated if he'd made the wrong assumption of her acquiescence. His concern elevated after he'd been home for two hours and no sign of her. Repeatedly, he paced to the living room to validate that her bag was still in the corner. He wore a path to the bathroom to check on her make-up, shampoo, and deodorant.

By eight, he stood on the back porch and watched her dark house like the peeping tom he'd exposed days earlier. A neighbor would surely notice. At eight-fifteen, Todd fired off a brief text. "You okay?"

"Yep. Great. See you later." *Sure. Thanks for explaining.*

"This is stupid," he muttered before returning to his computer and pulling up the orders for Monday. He delved into the work, forcing himself to take his mind off personal matters. The fact that he even had *personal matters* to think about pissed him off.

A soft whoosh signaled the front door easing closed just before the click of the lock acknowledged it. Todd was pleased he had finally been able to lose himself in work. Something that used to concern Annie, but Reva understood. Hell, he'd seen her entranced at the kitchen table with her head just above the keyboard.

He glanced down. The time on the taskbar of his flat screen said 11:42 p.m.

Friday night, out late. He realized he'd made a lot of assumptions when it came to Reva. It wasn't his business to know where she was or who she was with. Obviously her brothers did because they hadn't called and weren't at her house.

A shuffle signaled her proximity and he looked up with a scowl. She leaned against the doorjamb and watched. "You busy?"

"What do you think?" His voice, decidedly gruff, was almost a stab at the sweetness of her statement. She could have at least told him where she was so he wouldn't worry.

"I'll leave you alone then. Goodnight." She disappeared.

Children are immune to altitude and heat. Eric trudged up the granite outcropping with ease. His tireless march kept Reva on her toes as he pointed out every bug, lizard, and weed along the way. Too bad trees didn't grow on rock. More shade would have been nice.

Still, the child's constant chatter brought a smile to her lips as her lungs heaved from the fast pace. Even with all the jogging, she winded a bit. When they reached the top, the view of the surrounding area amazed her. She'd been there before but it had been years. She'd forgotten.

"Nice, isn't it?" Todd said from behind.

"I'd forgotten. I haven't been here in ages. I told some of the people at work about it and everyone agreed it was one of those great places to go that one always forgets. Look. You can see the river on the far side of the city. It's beautiful how the clouds almost hover. Do you do this often?"

"Three or four times a year. Eric likes it and it's a good way to spend a day. I don't have a lot of time with work or we might do it more often." Todd turned and set his backpack down to dig through it.

Reva yawned and stretched bare arms to the sky. She'd worn a tank top under her hoodie. The hoodie had come off in the first thirty minutes and was tied around her waist. The trek had warmed her almost as much as a morning run, with less stress on the knees. She was still tired though. She hadn't slept well.

Todd had been too busy to talk and she craved the discussion on her news. The conversation with her cousin, David, went well. It was always handy to have a lawyer in the family.

"Did you adopt Eric while you were married to Annie?" Todd twisted around and squinted into the sun at her. "That's random. Yes."

"Have you ever thought about talking with your attorney about her ultimatum?"

"I had a friend in college who went to law school. I talked with him a long time ago. He said since Eric's not my natural born child, it's unlikely I could challenge her on much of anything."

She frowned. "You need to meet my cousin, David."

"Why not? I've met the rest of your family. You hungry?" Reva glanced behind Todd to the blanket spread on the ground. He'd emptied his backpack of sandwiches, chips, and drinks.

"Dad, check out this lizard!" Eric stood over a bump of rocks, intently focused on the small life-form sunning. It watched him warily.

Reva didn't mention the situation further but she ground over it silently. She had to get David and Todd together. David had sounded pretty optimistic. Unfortunately, he also said it might get ugly. Todd said he didn't deal well with drama. From his comments, he'd had more than enough of that already. Ironically, she recognized the falseness behind his words. He dealt with it alright.

Three plus hours later, Reva trailed after Todd and Eric to their cars. They'd ridden separately so Todd could drop him home immediately after. He was annoyed that Reva insisted, but she had no intention of spoiling the outing with a nasty parental scene in front of the child. Now, as they meandered toward the end of the fun, she was pleased with her decision. Eric chattered away as they eased toward the parking lot, his fingers entwined in Todd's.

"I have to stop and get gas on the way back. See you at the house?" Todd asked.

"Maybe. I thought I'd go ahead and get my things and head home."

"In a hurry?" He glanced over the numerous cars parked around them as a family of four moved closer. Eric peered up, his head swiveled from one to the other.

"Nope. Eric, you need a drink? I thought I'd stop at the store by the park gate and get a water." Quick change of subject. "Yes, ma'am." He dropped Todd's hand and ran to their vehicle.

Todd reached a hand to slip Reva's wayward hair behind her ear. The simple act normally would have caused her to jump backward. Not so with him. "We'll follow you down."

The roll of his shoulders as he moved to his car brought further warmth to her already clammy skin. She slipped into her car and steered downhill to the store.

Inside, Eric ran to the restroom with Todd following. Reva grinned. She hated to admit it, but she couldn't help but enjoy a day like this, and the two of them as they bantered back and forth. The drinks were in refrigerated windows toward the back. She managed her way down the aisle and opened a door to extract three water bottles.

"Well, hey there, Reva!" a voice called behind her. Startled, she glanced up with the bottles balanced in her arms. Adam. She looked toward the bathroom.

"Hey, Adam. I didn't expect to see you here." She stepped back and let the door close, encapsulating the cool air that had felt so good on her face.

"Yeah, what a surprise," he admitted. "I was just up the road, bicycling with some friends." Adam waved a hand at the window and Reva noticed a truck outside with a bicycle's handlebars over the tailgate.

A coolness tingled along her skin and she glanced back to see if anyone had opened the fridge behind her. Nope.

"You're a biker?"

"On the weekends. It's good exercise and gets me outside." He glanced to the window. "Well, I'd better get going. See you Monday." He raised his hand with an energy bar grasped between fingers in a salute.

Reva followed until she reached the counter and paid for the bottles of water. Todd and Eric were still in the bathroom. She glanced at the door and could hear their voices in the small space. Amazing how long it takes for a little boy to go to the bathroom. Wasn't that only little girls? It would be easier to wait by the car rather than the small space between the aisles. With paper bag in hand, she pushed the door open.

Adam rolled over the engine of his truck. It sputtered and died. Reva waved and continued to her car. She heard the churning of the engine a few times, then the metal clang of the door shutting.

"Hey, Reva!" Adam called. "Wait up. I'm having trouble with my truck. Do you think you could give me a ride down to the bike trail so I can get one of my friends to help out?"

She glanced at the glass window, seeking Todd and Eric through the glass. *What's taking so long?*

"Um, I guess so. Can you give me just a minute to—"

"I should hurry before they all leave. It's real close."

Reva shrugged. "Sure. Hop in." The paper bag was tossed into the console and she slipped behind the wheel. She lifted her iPhone to peck in a message to Todd.

Adam grabbed it from her hand and slid his finger along the screen surveying the features. "You have one of the new ones. I've wanted one of those." He glanced up as they exited the lot and pointed toward a dirt road a quarter of a mile ahead. "Turn there. It's down at the end."

Reva watched him toss her phone in the back seat. *Shit.*

Todd came out of the bathroom practically growling with impatience. Eric, for all his mature conversations and playfulness, was still a little boy. He'd wet himself on the way to the bathroom. Couldn't hold it any longer, poor kid. Todd had noticed him squirming on the way down and twice suggested he take care of it behind a rock or the few scraggy bushes they'd passed. No. Too embarrassing in front of Reva. Fortunately, Todd had thought to bring a change of clothes in the backpack.

After working Eric out of the clothes, washing the skinny legs and body, and slipping on the clean undies, shirt and shorts—the kid was fine. Except for the dust all over his face, and dirt on his hands. Todd lifted him over the sink and propped Eric on a knee with the water running. A bit of soap added to the mix made sure that the face was once again clean and sparkling. Ten minutes later they walked out of the bathroom with the soiled clothes in a plastic bag.

"Dad, where's Ms. Reva?" Eric asked.

"She probably got tired of waiting and went outside." The jingle of the door as they exited caught his attention. He surveyed the lot. She'd left? Seriously?

He whipped the phone off the dashboard and sent a quick message.

Where'd you go?

No answer.

You okay? he added.

Nothing.

Eric skipped to the car. Todd walked back inside and looked around while Eric waited in the passenger seat. The jingle of the bells over the door eerily signaled his entrance and it occurred to him that he'd heard it twice while in the store. Reva had left. *Someone else too?*

The store clerk sat behind the counter watching a small television screen.

"Did you see a woman leave just a few minutes ago? Long brown hair, tank top and shorts?"

"Yeah. They took off down that way about five minutes ago." The man's tattooed finger pointed toward town.

THEY?

"She was with someone?"

"Sure. The guy she was with went with her. Why?"

"The guy she was with *was me*. Who did you see with her?"

"I don't know. Just some dude. Dark hair. Medium height. Dressed in bicycle gear." The clerk gestured to signify height and weight. "She knew him. They seemed okay."

"Did you get his name? Did she call him by name?"

"I don't know. I don't remember, but his truck wouldn't start and he ran out after her." The man gestured at the brown truck sitting in front of the window. Todd froze.

Dark windows. Brown truck. Taillights looked the same. *Shit. Shit.* He dialed Officer Teckley's number. Voicemail. *Dammit.* "Officer Teckley, this is Todd Grisham. I've got kind of a situation here. I think I found Reva's friend. Can you call me back right away? She might be in trouble." Todd ended the call and phoned Tim, Ben, and her parents.

Eons later, he'd rallied the group and realized that, for all their preparation, the plan to saturate the neighborhood and ward the guy off had failed. *He'd* failed. His iPhone buzzed into action and Todd jerked it to his ear.

"Todd." It was impossible to mask the impatience now.

"Wow. Having a bad time, sweetie?" Annie's voice surfaced a cringe.

"What do you want, Annie? I don't have time to talk."

"I just wanted to check on Eric. We're going out to eat tonight and I need him home asap."

Todd rolled his eyes. *Not now.* Eric sat in the car, glancing through the book he'd slid out from under the seat. He was completely unconcerned with Reva's disappearance.

"Sorry, but I can't bring him. I have something going on and I can't leave. You can come get him."

"You're addicted to your work, you know. That's why it never worked for us. I'll be over in thirty minutes."

"I'm not getting into an argument with you right now, Annie. I'm not at home. We're still at the park."

"Still at the park? And you can't even drop him by on your way home?" Her voice rose.

"Look, Reva's missing. I'm not leaving until the police get here and we can figure out what happened or she calls."

"Reva? She went *with you?*"

"Yes."

"But I told you—"

"And I am telling you, it's none of your business. *She's* none of your business. We're not discussing this. If you need Eric home, come get him. Otherwise, I'll drop him by as soon as I can. Reva's in trouble. Get it? Or don't you care?"

Todd hung up. He jogged to the street and peered both ways down the road, hoping to see her car. Nothing. The brightness of the sun glared off a broken glass down the street as if to wink at him. Sure, they were likely way gone by now but he could hope, right?

"Dad! Where're you going?"

He turned back to Eric. "I'm not going anywhere, bud. I was just checking for Reva's car." He looked at the cover of the book Eric held. Todd had an idea. "You remember those walkie talkies we used when you and Mom first moved around the corner?"

"The red and blue ones that I called you on before bedtime?" Eric asked.

"Yes! They're under the back seat of the car with the other stuff your mom gave me a while back." It wasn't time to explain that Annie had told him Eric needed more independence and his need to call Todd whenever he got scared had been a problem. "Can you get them?"

Eric pulled the car door. When it wouldn't budge, he leaned backward and yanked with both hands. Todd smiled despite his worry as the door gave way and his young son scrambled to get the toys.

"Got 'em." Eric held one up and pushed the button on the other. "They're not working, Dad." He shook them, then pushed the button again.

"The batteries are probably dead. Here, take this money in and get some new ones. The guy inside will help you. We're gonna need them." It was a big job for a little guy, but Eric was smart and puffed proudly with the trust he'd been given.

Minutes ticked off. Todd heard gravel spray as Ben's pickup flew into the parking lot and spun to a stop. Tim jumped out, followed by a petite blonde, then Ben.

"You find her?" Tim asked.

"Not yet. Cops are on the way though."

Sirens in the distance punctuated his statement. The blonde stepped forward and held out a hand. "I'm Ben's wife. Ben talks about you a lot."

Todd nodded. She swirled the bottled water in her hand and took a sip. He looked past her to Eric's small frame running toward him.

"I fixed them. Look." His big eyes beamed up as the child held out the walkie talkies. They both clicked into action and hissed as he pressed the buttons up and down. Wasn't it amazing how a small victory could boost a kid's confidence?

"I knew you would. Thanks. Now, listen up, son. I'm going down the road there and I need you to take this one. I'll take the other. We're going to play a game sort of. This is going to be the command post and you and Ben here are going to be in charge of it. Tim is going with me. Reva's hiding and we're going to find her, okay? You can be Ben's lieutenant."

Ben nodded when Todd lifted a brow his way. He understood. They had to get moving. If this guy, whoever he was, had her—they'd already given him too much time. He switched his gaze to Tim. "Let's go."

"Don't be surprised if we get out of range. I'll use the cell if there's a signal."

They scrambled into his Jeep and he careened it toward town. The patrol car whizzing by would have to talk to the others. No time for delay. He had no idea where to go or how to find her. He hated not having a plan. The man's truck was at the store so they couldn't be far, right? The sun glared off the broken glass he'd noticed earlier on the road and he swerved to miss it. The rearview mirror showed a bottle rolling to the grass by the pavement—not broken glass, a *water bottle*. A completely full water bottle.

He jerked the wheel and did a one-eighty. "What the hell?" Tim peered sideways.

"Look!" Todd pointed at the ruts that disappeared into the trees beyond where the bottle had slowed to rest. He grabbed the radio from the dashboard and clicked the button to call Ben and Eric. An unfamiliar voice said, "Here."

"Where are Eric and Ben?" The radio crackled when Todd released the button.

"They walked over to talk to the cops."

"Who are you?"

"I'm David, Reva's cousin. She's told me a lot about you."

"Yeah, well, she hasn't told me shit about you." Todd knew his patience wasn't making any friends but he didn't care.

"I'm the family lawyer."

"Good for you. Tell Ben we turned down the first dirt road on the right." Todd tossed the radio to the dashboard.

"I wouldn't get on his bad side just yet." Tim rolled down his window and the scent of leaves and dirt pelted in on them. "He's going to help you with Eric."

"No kidding. How's he going to do that?" Todd checked the rearview but dust clouded so high it wasn't possible to see.

"You'd be surprised what David can do. He's a pit bull when it comes to the law and Reva spent most of last night telling him what a great Dad you are. Since David's divorced and only sees his kids once a month, you're his next big case.

He has a soft spot for kids. And dads."

Well,hell.

CHAPTER TWENTY SIX

Reva took a sip from the bottle of water and rested her arm on the open window. The day was still young but the trees blocked the afternoon sun. As she lifted the bottle for a second sip it slipped from her hand. She reached down to grab it, saw the bag from the store, and tossed both out the window.

She slid a glance toward Adam. "There're bike trails down here?" she asked.

"Yeah, it gets a little rough, but when you get closer to the river it opens up and there's a lot of trails along the water and up into the trees. It's more for mountain biking, not street bikes. You ever do any of that?"

"No. I jog. Never took up cycling. I'm not sure why, I just didn't. I think it's cool that you do that though."

"You play softball too."

"Yes." She remembered when she'd been in a hurry to get to practice. "So, were there a lot of people out here today? I don't see any cars or bikes."

"Just my group. Not many. Turn up there where the tire tracks are."

She gulped down the last of the second water and tossed it out the window as she spun the wheel. It was a long shot but she had nothing else to use. From what she saw, very few traveled this way. What possessed a person to take off on a deserted road just on a whim?

"You shouldn't litter."

"It'll deteriorate. Those new bottles are biodegradable."

"Yeah, in a hundred years." His voice grated. The birds chattered away in the trees. A siren in the distance increased in volume to signify an emergency vehicle approaching. Adam rested an arm over the seat and glanced back. "Must be a fire somewhere."

"Hope not. We're right in the middle of a forest full of dry trees in the middle of a drought. How far is this place where your friends are?"

"Just up there." He pointed at an opening in the trees where a dock extended over river water that barely rippled.

Reva pulled to a stop just clear of the trees and got out. The only sounds were birds and wind rustling through the leaves. Adam stepped out also and walked toward the dock. She thought it odd that he wore a fanny pack on his hips. *Didn't those go out of style years ago?*

"They've already gone," he said without turning back. "So, what do we do now?"

"I can take you back to the store. My friends are waiting for me."

He whirled around. "Who? There wasn't anyone with you."

"They were in the bathroom."

He nodded and she knew he didn't believe a word. Adam smiled and strode toward her. "So, what is it with you and me, Reva?"

"Huh? There is no you and me. What are you talking about?"

"Why is that? You obviously are attractive and so am I. Haven't you thought about it?" Adam stepped in a bit too close.

Reva went into her protective mode. She stared down and kept a monitored awareness of his movements. "Off limits, Adam. I'm your boss. But since you're asking—no, I hadn't thought about it."

"Never?"

"Never."

"Why not? You're fairly active, socially."

"What?" Her eyes shot up. *Active?*

"Well, you date a lot. If that's what it is." The chill of his forefinger trailing down her arm caused a shiver. She stepped back. Her shoe crunched on dried leaves and twigs underneath.

"How do you know whether I date or not? That's none of your business."

"I've noticed."

The only way he would possibly notice something like that would be if he had watched. *He had watched.* With another step backward, Reva glanced into the trees on both sides. The birds ceased their chatter as if sensing a pending storm. The silence punctuated his movement as Adam clamped a hand around Reva's forearm.

"Adam, let go. We need to get back. My friends will be concerned."

He laughed a single snort but dropped his grip. "Yeah, right. There's no one back there. And we're going to stay right here. It's kind of romantic, don't you think?"

No. No. Not Romantic. Not a bicycle trail. Not even safe. Reva's gaze swiveled again to the trees, searching for an escape. She glanced back at her car. She'd left the door open, keys in her pocket. Unfortunately, his door was also wedged open and ready.

"I'm going back," she announced. "You can either go or stay. That's up to you." She turned and tromped three steps toward the car. Three steps that took great strength and escalated the tension building in her gut.

"Why do you hate me so much? Are you afraid I'm better than you? That I'd actually do a better job? They all like me, you know. At the office. They like me a lot more than you because I can talk and joke with everyone. And I make sense when I talk about the project. I don't try to over-explain or condescend like you do."

She kept moving. Step. Step. Step. One after the other, slowly so that it didn't alarm him. The crunch of his feet on the ground behind her kept pace. "I don't hate you, Adam. You're an employee. Your success is important to mine. We're too big of an organization for it to only be about one individual." She felt the cold metal of the keys in her pocket but held them still so he wouldn't hear.

"The truth is, Reva, dear," Adam said, "I don't really care

about anyone else's success. Neither do you. You only care about you. That's why we belong together. We're the same, you and I."

Adam strutted past and shoved the car door closed. The thump sent a few birds fluttering above. The crunch of tires against the dirt and gravel road caught his attention. They both turned and squinted behind her car. The rumble of a motor signaled an approaching vehicle. Adam growled.

Through the fading light behind the trees, Reva made out the shape of a truck bumping along the ruts of the road. The engine revved and sped closer as if the passengers had seen them too.

"Your friends?" she asked before she recognized the vehicle color and silhouettes inside. *No, mine.* Relief almost made her giddy. It definitely warmed the cold feeling that had started through her shoulders.

Todd saw the light glance off Reva's car before they were close enough to recognize anything else.

"Look," Tim acknowledged, as he pointed at the beam of light flickering between the trees. "There's a car."

The truck bumped over the worn ruts in the dirt path that had once held gravel. As they eased closer Todd made out the outline of two people on the other side of the vehicle. A man and woman. The woman looked over her shoulder at their approaching vehicle. The simple gesture confirmed what he already knew. Todd pressed the gas and lunged the vehicle forward over the remaining bumps and ruts. He didn't care that it bounced Tim's head against the roof, nor did he care that something in the back of the pickup clanged loudly.

"Call back and let them know." Todd tossed the radio at Tim, flung the truck into park, and leapt out before it stopped rolling. Reva stood close to the man. He had one hand behind his back and the other at his side. Todd didn't miss the fact that he'd dropped it from her arm only seconds earlier when they appeared through the trees. He squinted to take in Reva's face as he approached.

"Everything okay here?" Todd asked, not shifting his gaze from her.

The guy shook his head. "Naw, we're good. I just had a little car trouble and my friend here was trying to help."

The guy had no idea that Reva knew their new visitors. Apparently, he thought they'd just happened onto the scene. Tim had finished his call on the radio and stepped out of the truck, rounded the corner, and came forward with his hands in his pockets.

"Todd, did you know there's a target shooting gallery over in those trees? I saw it while I was talking to Ben." Tim pointed at a series of small white targets nailed to the tree trunks in the woods. "We should come out here sometime."

The guy looked from Todd to Tim, then back. He smiled. "I come out on the weekends sometimes by myself. It's pretty peaceful. The bike trails go along the river bank though so you have to be careful not to shoot someone."

The stranger wiped his hand on his shirt and reached toward them. "I'm Adam and this is my friend, Reva."

Reva's face clouded. Tim studied the guy without offering his hand. "You know her?" Tim asked, "How?"

Todd noticed the startled expression that crossed Adam's eyes as well as Reva's stillness.

"We work together," Adam answered. "Right Reva?"

"Uh, right." She slowly stepped forward, a stilted silent glide toward Todd. Todd flicked an eye at the man as he started for her hand, then stopped. "Adam's friends were supposed to be here and give him a ride but they've already gone. You'll be okay though, right?"

She glanced back over her shoulder and offered a grim smile before she slipped her fingers into Todd's. The iciness of her skin cooled his palm and he was thankful they'd found her. He leaned into her hair and whispered. "You scared me. Sure you're okay?"

She nodded and waited for Adam's response. He watched the three, realizing the error in his assumption that the truck held random passers-by. "Yeah, sure. I'll just call and get one of them to come back. No problem. Thanks for trying, boss. I appreciate it. You guys go ahead." He brushed his hand at them in a dismissing gesture. The smell of pine reached Todd's nose, along with a muskier tone. There must be a dead raccoon or something nearby. He recognized the scent of decay.

Todd let Reva slip into the seat between he and Tim, then climbed in behind. Adam stood watching them, hands on hips. A cloud passed across his face and Todd knew there was more to the story than either of them had described. The rearview mirror displayed Adam for easy view as they bounced away over the rutted road. Adam turned his back to them and passed a hand through his hair, a movement that Todd had witnessed once before. Todd frowned.

"He's more than just a coworker, isn't he?" he asked.

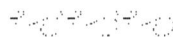

Reva darted eyes sideways. "Excuse me?"

Surely he didn't think there was something going on with Adam?

"How well do you know that guy?" The calm tone didn't do anything to hide the inference. He did. As if there hadn't been enough to add to the tension in her life, now this. Reva wanted to scream.

"Look, I work with him. That's all. If you think there's something else going on, that's *your* problem, not mine. What the hell is wrong with men that they automatically think there has to be something more than just a work relationship? Can't you see what he was doing? Do you *really* think I'd be interested in that guy? You know what...why don't you and he have a long talk. You both deserve each other." She hooked a finger at the barely distinguishable figure in the back window. She lifted her hip to pull whatever was jabbing her in the butt out from underneath. A walkie-talkie.

Todd glanced at the device in her hand. "We were talking to Eric and Ben. Only they didn't answer. Some cousin of yours was there."

"David," Tim interjected, "they're waiting for us back at the store." Tim's hands were hanging between his knees. He dropped something on the floor and kicked it under the seat then readjusted to give her room.

"So, we have the whole family out here?" She breathed in deeply. They had rounded the small twist in the road and the pavement of the highway quickly approached. The smell of dust and pine filtrated into her head. Todd's fingers were white on the steering wheel. *They had a search party out for me.*

Todd shrugged. "You disappeared without a sound, so I called your brothers. And I called the police."

CHAPTER TWENTY SEVEN

———   ———

*N*ow *what?* Adam stood watching the truck disappear. Silently, he thanked whatever force compelled them to leave without lingering. The last thing needed at this point was an outdoor adventure by her group tramping around in areas he preferred left alone. They saw the target practice site, he reminded himself. No biggie. There's no law against having a gun, nor in learning to shoot it.

Fortunately, they didn't find what was beyond the targets.

He'd said too much though. Things would get difficult at work. Admittedly, the comments weren't appropriate but he *knew* she understood. They *were* alike. That's probably why she'd been so hard on him in the office. Well, she'd just have to get past that. He'd managed to charm the others—he could manage her too. And, if he couldn't, then he'd just make sure the others trusted him more, believed him more. Either way, he'd conquer this mountain. With or without her. She was *not* standing in his way again. Not this time. Not ever again.

Adam felt behind his back to make sure he'd left the pouch zipped. Yes. Good. He pulled it from his waist, removed the contents and headed toward the target in the trees. It was probably best to stash it and take the shortcut through the woods to get his truck. He needed to kill some time anyway before the commotion at the convenience store cleared. On the off chance that they came looking for him, there was a lot of undergrowth to conceal his travels.

And they did. Come looking for him, that is.

He heard the grumble of two engines and, from his perch several hundred yards away in the brush, he saw tracks of dust cloud puff through the trees. It surprised him a little to see two cop cars, but not so much as to panic and run. The officers walked around a bit, called out, then left.

This was a good spot to watch. He could see the road in front of the store plus the opening with the dock. He expected to wait long enough to ensure Reva and her friends were gone, then hustle up to get his truck. The cops added a new element he needed to think about. While he'd had a clean record up to this point, he doubted he'd be able to speak with them calmly.

When the last of the sun's beam flittered down behind the trees, the glow in the sky cast some fairly ominous shadows. Adam noticed that the noise of cicadas and other unknown life kicked up a notch. His ears rang with it. Several cars left the store and headed back toward the city but he stayed put. The lights from inside the store cast a yellow stain across the lot and out into the road.

He perched in his cocoon of underbrush and waited until the lights clicked off and darkness engulfed the road. When a lone set of headlights left the store and headed down the road, he decided it was okay to move.

But not in that truck. He only had a few hours before it would all erupt.

CHAPTER TWENTY EIGHT

A dam considered his options for the umpteenth time on the short trek to his house. None of them panned out in his mind the way he needed. Admittedly, he'd crossed the line. Not just crossed it, he was practically across the continent from it. Why had she pushed him so far? He'd never wanted to react like that. He wasn't a violent man. He didn't do that type of thing.

He strung his fingers through his hair. One of the men that came for Reva had directed the cops to his truck. Adam had watched as they took the license and walked around, surveying his new vehicle as if it were—evidence.

Shit.

It was like watching an episode of CSI as they stalked around, surveying the vehicle, running hands along the bed. *They knew.* He was screwed. He had to get out. Go away. Forget work, he needed a new life. *Damn Reva.* She could have just left him alone and none of this would have happened. The project would have been completed by now. And he'd have been virtually in command. Of everything. No, she had to be a bitch about it.

It had taken forty minutes to jog the five miles to his house. Thank God it was such a short distance. Trying to hurry in the trails through the trees had been tricky. He could have made it faster on the road but didn't want to risk being seen.

Inside the house, Adam grabbed his backpack from the closet. He filled it with supplies, tossed in his gun and clips, then headed out the back door. Can't let the neighbors see him leave. The time on his watch told him an hour had passed. He needed a vehicle and planned to make one last stop before saying adios to this town. There was a thrill to starting over. He'd never done it before. Not like this.

Adam left his neighbor's "borrowed" van at the park near Reva's house. A quick jog put him in the backyard where he'd watched her a few times before. The house was dark. He turned to view the other house where the cell phone had nearly exposed him. Dark too.

He skipped the doors and pried a window to one of the back rooms open with his pocketknife. Once inside, a quick scan of the rooms told him she was still out. The woman had quite the social life. He hunched into an easy chair in her living room, dropped the bag on the floor at his feet, and clutched the weapon in his lap. He'd just wait for her return. No rush now. This was the last item he needed to take care of before moving on.

A loud rap on the door startled him awake. He glanced at his watch. Too dark to read it but the glow-in-the-dark hands told him it was around nine ten. He swiped a hand down his face. No need to answer the door since it wasn't his house.

A scratching noise caught his attention. Someone else wanted in? Without a key? *No way.* He stood and looked from side to side for a good spot to conceal his presence. The door swung open and a big man with a burr head stepped in.

"Stop right there," Adam commanded. He raised the run. There was enough light in the room to see the shock on the man's face.

"Hang on now. Who are you? " The man held up his hands. "I'm not here to cause trouble. I just wanted to talk to Reva."

Burrhead wore a starched shirt and slacks as if he were a salesman making a call. *At this time of night?* Not likely. A motor's whirring signaled an arrival out front. Adam peeked at the glass to see Reva's car.

Reva had given up the driver's seat to Todd at his insistence. If he wanted to drive, fine. She'd only grumbled a smidge because the day had been so tiring she really didn't care. She felt cocooned between the two bulky men beside her and her brothers and Eric in the back. Her Dad had insisted on riding along until they were at Todd's. She glanced from one solemn face to another.

"Do you ever wonder what makes a person decide to be violent?" She blew upward to ruffle the bangs out of her eyes, her hands were pinned to her sides. "I mean, think about it, one day a person seems completely charming and normal. Then without any warning, something sets him off. Out of nowhere."

Both men in the front seat shot her a look as they turned into her drive. Neither spoke. She knew they weren't sure whether she really wanted their opinion or not.

"Only it's not really out of nowhere, is it? Something triggers it but you don't know what it is. You don't even know there's a problem. You just wander through your day, thinking everything's all great. Then *wham*. " Reva pushed a shoulder into her father. "Let me out Dad, and I'll run in and get my stuff. You guys can stay here. I won't be a minute. Eric, you want to go? We'll get the paint and maybe we can paint a shirt or something tonight?"

She placed a shaky hand over the back of the seat. Todd noticed. They all probably did. Reva needed to stay busy and nothing like a five-year old boy to keep one distracted from personal issues.

"Sure," Eric answered as he crawled up on the seat. By the time Tim had pulled the handle on the door, Eric had already scurried over the seat and dropped his legs to the ground. "Be right back." He grinned at Todd.

"We'll grab your lawn chairs from the backyard." Todd slipped from the car with Ben and Tim alongside and headed to the gate. "You probably don't want to do that inside and I don't have anywhere to manage it-we can spread it across the chairs."

Reva took Eric's hand and they swung arms as they pranced up the steps to the door. They were already at the threshold when she looked up to see the door ajar with a man's back to her. A chill cursed through her, causing an abrupt stillness. A man she had hoped to never see again. Nick. *What the hell?* She clenched down on Eric's hand but it was too late. He'd already slipped past her and ran through.

"Come on in, boss."

Adam.

Reva swallowed hard and started to motion to the car.

"No, I said come in, now. Don't make me get ugly." Adam tilted the gun just a hair, then narrowed his eyes. He was comfortable with the weapon, no doubt. Not a good idea to challenge that and find out.

"Adam," she stated flatly as she swiveled from one man to the other, "and Nick. What's going on?"

"Good question," Adam answered.

Nick glared. "You put a *restraining order* on me, Reva? On me? Looks like you have bigger issues than someone that's halfway around the damn globe." Nick nodded at the firearm staring them down. "Don't you think you have the wrong guy? They served me at my apartment, right in front of Jessie."

Reva assumed Jessie was the new girlfriend. "You sent me hate mail."

"I didn't send you shit. You left. I moved on."

"Who the hell are you?" Adam thrust the gun toward Nick.

"The fiancé."

"*Ex*-fiancé and why are you here? You didn't fly all the way here just because of a restraining order." Reva glared. She desperately tried to ignore Adam's shaking hand on the firearm.

"You had me arrested, then ran out in the middle of the night to God knows where. After no word for all this time, you decide to slap a restraining order on me. What the hell?"

The clip-clop of heels on the concrete walk in front, signaled another woman's approach.

"Shut up. Don't move," Adam hissed.

Clump. Clump. Clump. The heels mounted the steps and tromped to the door. Reva could feel Eric's tiny form snugged against her legs. His fingers bit into her thigh.

"Hello?" A female voice. "Reva Zamora? Are you there?"

The streetlight behind the fading sun cast an iridescent glow on the short-cropped blonde hair of the woman as she tilted her head in the door. Damn.

"Who the fuck are you?" Adam asked.

Annie flung her hands into the air and evaluated the room. Nick with hands up, Reva with Eric tucked in behind her, one hand on his shoulder, and some unknown crazy man flailing a gun at everyone. Reva could feel the disapproval in her fear-laced glare. "Holy shit! I'm no one. I'm just the wife of her neighbor and I want my kid."

"Ex-wife," Reva corrected, "of my neighbor."

"The peeping tom in the backyard?"

While the others were distracted with Annie's appearance Reva slipped her cell and Officer Teckley's card into Eric's hand. She looked down and mouthed *Go call*. Then gave Eric a small shove down the hall toward the back of the house.

Crack. She turned back to see Nick fling himself on Adam. The gun had gone off but she couldn't tell whether he'd been hit or not. He tossed out a few curses and landed heavy on Adam's chest, knocking both to the floor. The gun dislodged and tumbled across the carpet. Nick took the opportunity to straddle Adam, then started pummeling him with bare fists. Bones crunched, flesh turned to raw steak, and Reva could hardly see Adam's eyes or nose for all the blood.

Fabric ripped. The starched shirt tail pulled loose from Nick's waistband. He's really not going to like that, she thought. Then she noticed the blood drips seeping through the fabric.

A voice boomed from the open door. "Oh, hell no. You're not doing that again!" Reva's Dad barreled into the room, grasped Nick's head in a vice grip and yanked back.

"Hey!" Nick yelled.

"You are not *ever* beating on one of my kids ever again, you piece of shit." José Zamora held tight, and dragged Nick away from Adam. Nick went limp in his arms and sagged to the floor. Reva hadn't seen the hole in his shirt from behind, she'd registered the blood but thought it was Adam's. The stain of blood seeping through the shirt told her otherwise.

"He's shot, Dad," she mumbled. "Let him go."

Adam flailed around for his handgun but the blood in his eyes seemed to make it hard to find.

"Looking for something?" Todd's voice called from his back. Reva hadn't seen him come in. Hadn't seen him creep around Nick. Yet, there he stood with the gun pointed dead at the man's eyes. "I'd recommend you calm down and have a seat."

The sound of sirens in the distance sent a relieved sag through Reva's shoulders. Eric had called. Thank God.

"Todd, what the hell is going on, and where is my son?" Annie yelled. "Who *are these people* and what have you gotten yourself into with this crazy woman?" The fear in her eyes was replaced with fury. "Eric, get out here! We're leaving."

"He's not here, Annie."

"Yes, he is. He came in with that bitch." Her finger jammed at Reva.

"He climbed out the window and came and got me in the backyard right after he called 911. I sent him over the fence to my house and came back. He's fine, but he's not here."

"You're done playing Dad with my son, Todd. I don't know what kind of crazy—"

"Shut up Annie. I'm not *playing* Dad, I *am* his Dad. Don't you remember the adoption papers? I'm the only dad Eric knows and you should be glad about that, since you have to be the shittiest mother on earth."

"How *dare*—" Annie started.

"No! How dare you. Dumping your kid off like a sack of groceries whenever you want to go have some fun with your married boyfriend. Not even checking to see if he's okay. Did you see what Reva did? Did you see—"

"Yeah, I saw. She put my son in front of some crazy man with a gun."

"*Our* son. And she *saved* him from the crazy man with a gun, in case you didn't notice. What the hell is wrong with you that you can't understand how to be a mother? Or a wife?"

"I—"

Todd's shoulders drooped. "Just stop, Annie. Just stop."

Officer Teckley and his crew swarmed the room, cuffed Adam, and called an ambulance for Nick. Great, Reva thought, we spent most of the evening giving statements and now we go back and do it again.

"Hey Todd." She waited for him to cross the room to her. He'd handed the gun to Teckley as soon as possible and stood back while the others did their jobs.

Todd pulled Reva in and hugged her. "You okay?"

"Yeah, but do you mind if we just do something normal and boring next time you want to impress me? You know, like maybe grill burgers in the backyard or order KFC?"

He stared at her and she knew he couldn't muster a laugh, though she'd tried to lighten the moment. He clenched his eyes for a second, then opened them and lifted a lip in a forced grin. "I guess we could do that."

The police hefted Adam to his feet and started to escort him to a waiting squad car.

"Adam?" Reva summoned.

"What."

She felt the coldness in his body language. Every nerve – ice cold. "You are *so fired.*"

CHAPTER TWENTY NINE

——— ———

Reva was pretty good at running away from places that held bad memories. She'd learned that when she escaped from Nick. It had been four weeks since the police handcuffed Adam and took him away.

He had been charged with murder. Two counts apparently and Reva was stunned. His truck apparently had dna evidence that pointed to the disappearance of a woman. She'd seen it on the news for days and was stunned when they connected it back to Adam. Once in custody, Adam had confessed and explained it as an accident. Reva was saddened that she hadn't seen the depths of darkness and anger during the time he worked for her. Sure, she had feared him a little, but she thought it was a result of her own issues, not his. Nick's death came as a shock at first.

 Nick had not survived the surgery to repair his gunshot wound. He'd lost too much blood. The doctors had been a little surprised that he'd been weakened so by the shot.It had not appeared life threatening. Apparently, he had some blood deformity that introduced complications. Reva's sadness was short-lived. Relief seemed more appropriate and she hated that she had such brief remorse at the loss. After all, she'd loved the man once. Hadn't she?

Looking at the obituary, she realized there was little love in the partnership they'd formed. It had been forged in fear and servitude. It had been difficult to call the girlfriend and inform her of his death. After multiple attempts where she'd hung up before an answer, she finally rang through to a voice. The girlfriend had disappeared and forwarded his phone to his office. Like Reva, she'd taken the opportunity to save herself. Reva wanted to applaud the bravery. Instead, it made her sad. How many other lives had Nick tortured? And who had done it to him?

She walked to the front door with Todd at her side. His truck behind them was filled with boxes ready to be packed full. She'd not spend another night alone in this house. Reva sighed.

"Does it make you sad to leave?" Todd asked.

"Not really. It's more of a cleansing. A chance to finally wash the uglies out of my life."

"That's a good way to look at it. I wish you'd stay with *me* though."

Reva touched his cheek. He leaned into her hand. She understood that this slight gesture meant something to him, the gentle stroke across his shadowed jaw. He'd said as much when they sprawled across his tangled sheets last night. When he'd asked her again to move in.

"Give me a little time, okay?"

He clasped the fingers and pressed them to his lips. "You got it."

They lugged boxes inside and spent the next three hours stuffing them full. It amazed Reva how much junk she'd collected in the short time she'd been in the house. Sweat trickled between her shoulder blades, tickling against her spine. A grumble in her stomach encouraged her to check her watch. It was almost one!

The clip clop of heels on the concrete signaled someone's arrival. "Yoo hoo. Reva?"

Reva turned to share an annoyed look with Todd.

"Dammit, Annie, can't you leave the girl alone?" he said when the bobbed blonde tromped in the open door, shadowed by Reva's cousin, David.

David hesitated on the threshold, nodding at both occupants. "I have some good news for you. We've come to a—" He placed a palm on Annie's shoulder and squeezed before continuing, "We've worked things out. I thought you'd want to know."

Todd and Reva shared another startled exchange.

"Yeah," Annie added, "David and I have spent a lot of time trying to come to some sort of compromise about your time with Eric." Annie fumbled with the button on the bottom of her too-tight blouse.

David grinned. "Just tell them, sweetie. They need to know."

Sweetie?

"See, I haven't been exactly straight about Bob. I'm not really seeing him. He dumped me eight months after I left you, Todd. He never really intended to leave his wife and marry me. He just said that to—well, you know." Annie bit into her lip and worked it hard. Reva thought her eyes glistened a bit as if a tear might drop. "He thought it was the perfect setup with me being married too. What an ass. I just couldn't say anything. I'd really screwed up. I was so stupid. So, I kept coming over and dropping Eric off. Sometimes because he wanted to see you and sometimes because I needed to be alone."

The puddle in her eye gave way to a couple of tears that rolled down and ruined her perfect make-up. Reva reluctantly felt her heart tug.

"Go on," David prompted.

"I didn't want Eric to see me crying all the time so if I couldn't face you, I'd just drop him and go home. I'd crawl in bed and cry. I was so mad. I didn't dare tell you but I thought I wanted you back. Only I knew you'd never have it, Todd. In a way, I also knew that wasn't right for either of us. Then you met Reva."

Reva turned and plunked a stack of books into the box behind her. Her face started to warm. *Here it comes.*

"I could see you really cared for her and it made me jealous and well, more lonely."

David cleared his throat and rubbed her shoulder. "Todd, what Annie's agreed to is this: Eric will stay with you during the summers and every other weekend, unless you can't take him. He'll stay with Annie during the school year. If you'd rather do it differently, she's open to ideas."

Annie hiccupped and Reva turned to see Annie's make-up smeared face watching her. "I'm sorry Reva. You saved Eric's life and I never really thanked you. I was so angry at myself and how badly I'd botched everything up, I just saw you..."

"As the bitch who'd weaseled into your family?" Reva grinned.

Annie giggled. "Well, yeah."

All four adults stood staring at the floor for endless minutes until the back door flung open. Eric swept in and hugged Todd, then Reva. "Dad, how are you gonna box up all that stuff in the backyard?" he asked.

Annie seemed to welcome the interruption that broke their tension. "What stuff is that, sweetie?"

David groaned. "Not you, too, Reva? Ben's filled your yard up with all that junk?"

Reva laughed. "Hey, now. It's art. Some of it isn't all that bad either. In fact, he's sold a few pieces to Todd's company. They're putting it in their catalog this fall."

"Good." David looked at Todd. "Maybe you can buy all mine too then." He grabbed a box and started loading it from the kitchen cabinets. Annie joined him and rubbed a hand across his back. Well, well. *Looks like they worked out more than just Todd's parental rights.*

Todd leaned into Reva's hair, his breath warm against her ear, and whispered. "He could do a lot worse, I guess."

She turned and kissed the corner of his mouth. "Yeah, they're cute. Who would have thought *that?*"

Eric flipped on Reva's music and pressed the button that she'd programmed to Disney tunes for him when they'd painted shirts. He grabbed a box and joined the packing party, though he danced more than packed. Within thirty minutes, the small team had moved to the bedroom when voices calling caught their attention.

"Where's the party?" That had to be Ben.

"Back here," Todd called. He and Reva went out to meet him. Only it wasn't just Ben. No, Ben, his kids, Tim, and Reva's parents all strolled in.

Reva's mom held a big bucket of KFC. "I thought you guys might be hungry." She smiled.

"You're an angel." Todd hugged her, covering her forehead in sweat. He swiped the boxes off the table and grabbed paper plates.

"Hey, David! Why don't you guys get in here and see this." Some scuffling in the back occurred, then David and Annie appeared.

"What's up? Oh, food! Whew, thanks."

Todd motioned to Reva. "Hey, gorgeous, why don't you dish it up for everyone?"

"Are you really trying to get me to serve food to this group? I think they can handle it themselves. I'm not your waitress," Reva huffed. She picked up a plate. "But I'll go first if you don't mind."

She slipped the lid off the chicken and started to reach in when her fingers touched—fuzz.

"What the?" A felt box. She stared down at it, befuddled. A breeze hit her sweaty legs as Todd dropped down next to her.

"So, what do you say, babe? Think you and I could do it right this time?" He glanced over his shoulder at Annie. "No offense, Annie."

"None taken." Still, there were tears in her eyes.

Reva looked at the box, then at the man on his knee in front of her. "Todd Grisham, are you proposing to me with a box of chicken? Seriously?"

He laughed. The whole room clapped. Her family roared with laughter. All of them. "Yes, honey, that's exactly what I'm doing. I'm being *normal*. Straight up normal and I'm asking you to be boringly and exquisitely average with me for the rest of your life. Right here. In front of your whole family. With this ring and a box of chicken. And I promise I won't lay a hand on you if you turn me down." Todd crossed fingers over his heart and held them up, then stood.

He lifted the box out of the chicken and brushed the crumbs away, then opened it and placed it in her hand. "So, what do you say?"

She smiled around the room. *Yes, this is how it was intended to be. Everyone around for all the big moments. Nothing hidden in the dark or behind closed doors. This is how someone loves you. And you love them.*

She gulped down the knot in her throat and took the ring out. "Wow, that Datemydad.com website really works!"

ABOUT THE AUTHOR

Shelley grew up on a farm outside of Kansas City, Missouri. She's a graduate of Oklahoma State University with a bit of post-graduate work at OSU and University of Wyoming-Casper. She now resides near Houston with her family.

OTHER TITLES BY SHELLEY K WALL INCLUDE:

Numbers Never Lie
Bring It On
The Designated Driver's Club

For a more current list, go to www.shelleykwall.com

www.ingramcontent.com/pod-product-compliance
Lightning Source LLC
Chambersburg PA
CBHW060927120626
46557CB00003B/902